Harem boy might not be the most appropriate role for someone who's never really seen the appeal of sex, but Elin's status as dahabi: golden in a land of tan and brown, has marked him for The Dragon's service since birth. He's content enough with his life of uncomplicated, if restrictive, luxury, until an unremarkable chore becomes a case of love at first sight.

Mysterious newcomer Hathar, a roguish "merchant adventurer" from far-off lands, ignites an exploration of Elin's first taste of physical desire, as well as a desire to experience life beyond the palace. Now, they must find a way to escape before Hathar's ship departs, stranding them forever in The Dragon's harem.

This is a work of fiction. All characters, places and events are from the author's imagination and should not be confused with fact. Any resemblance to persons, living or dead, events or places is purely coincidental.

Published by
NineStar Press
PO Box 91792
Albuquerque, New Mexico, 87199
www.ninestarpress.com

Warning: This book contains sexually explicit content, which is only suitable for mature readers.

Print ISBN # 978-1-947139-92-3
Cover by Natasha Snow
Edited by Elizabetta

GOLDEN

R.L. Mosswood

With thanks to Ayees, Liv, Alysa, and Cal for all their help and patience.

Chapter One

ELIN WOKE IN his usual place on the silken pallet between Nikil and Rian. The haram was dark, and the night sky outside the elegant, grated windows was still inky. He wasn't sure what had roused him. He couldn't recall a dream, and the room was quiet but for the usual nighttime chorus of the men's sighs and snores.

A moment later, he realized he could hear something else. Not in the room, but maybe down the hall or from the floor below, he could make out rough, raised voices. A fight? But who would it be at this hour, and in this part of the palace? He propped himself on his elbows a little and scanned the room—all the beds seemed to be filled. The men of the haram knew better than to fight anyway, at least not *that* kind of fighting, with yelling and tussling. The Dragon didn't take damage to "her boys" lightly, and anyone caught inflicting that damage was likely to disappear without notice or explanation.

He listened a little longer, trying to make out words or recognize a voice, but whatever was happening was far enough off to make that impossible. Finally, he heard a door slam, and that seemed to be the end of it.

He rolled over and drifted off, still puzzling over what he had heard.

AT BREAKFAST THE following morning, everything seemed normal. The hall was filled with the groggy murmur of men beginning their day, the rich aroma of coffee, and the tap of wooden cutlery on fine china.

Elin, as usual, sat on his own, thoughtfully chewing a honeyed pastry. Though it was hard to ever be truly *alone* in the haram, his tendency to quiet contemplation left him out of most of the livelier interactions the other men favored. He wasn't much for sport, which was one of the main entertainments among his comrades, and his thoughts tended to follow slow and dreamy pathways that didn't lend themselves to clever banter.

As he was pondering the particular play of light on the grain of the highly polished tabletop, a shadow moved into his peripheral vision. One of the guards, a man named Emun, was approaching. The guards of the haram were in a unique position: They were, in most ways, subordinate to the residents they guarded, so they spoke in polite tones, made requests rather than demands, and would usually do whatever was asked of them. At the same time, they were in charge of keeping the men in their place—generally not a hard job. Who would want to escape the lap of luxury, after all? But it was known that, if pushed, the guards would muster force to keep order, which lent an edge to all their interactions with their charges.

Elin finished his bite and looked up, inviting Emun to address him.

"I've got something for you to do after breakfast," he said. "A new resident who needs some cleaning up."

"A new resident? To our wing?"

Elin was used to being assigned chores considered beneath the more favored men of the haram, but this was unusual. His wing was inhabited by the twenty-one- to thirty-year-olds. They had all entered the haram as children, as soon as they'd been found by The Dragon's collectors, or ceded by their parents. New arrivals had trickled in through their younger years, a few carefully hidden late arrivals into their early teens, but it had been nearly a decade since anyone had joined the group Elin had grown up with.

"Yep." Emun cut his thoughts short. "City guard found him skulking around the palace walls and assumed he was an escapee, but we've never seen him before. He's The Dragon's now, of course. Pretty rough around the edges though. Weird accent, needs a scrub and a shave. See what you can do. Jurah will have him waiting for you outside the baths after you're done here."

"Sure. Okay." Elin wasn't sure what else to say. How did a fully grown *dahabi* end up wandering outside the palace? Did he mean to get caught? He supposed he'd have a chance to answer all his questions soon enough, and returned to his breakfast as Emun returned to his post near the door.

OUTSIDE THE BATHS, Jurah was waiting as promised. With the guard was a man who could only be the new addition, looking much worse for wear than Elin had anticipated. His hair was so filthy and matted that Elin was surprised the city guard had known him as *dahabi* at all, and there was blood caked down his cheek and through his stubble from an angry split on his brow. He hadn't come voluntarily, then. The sturdy rope binding the man's wrists only reinforced that fact.

"Emun asked me to come down after breakfast," he said, not quite ready to volunteer what he'd been asked to do. Maybe Jurah had a different understanding of the matter.

No such luck. "Yeah! I've got quite a job for you here," the guard replied jovially, indicating the filthy man by tugging lightly on his bindings. The "job" in question scowled slightly, but said nothing.

"Does he, uh, need to stay bound like that?" Helping with a bath was one thing, but Elin didn't think he had it in him to wrestle anyone into submission.

"Oh, no. Our friend here has settled down quite a bit since last night. He's going to be on his best behavior for you. Right?" With that, Jurah elbowed the other man for a reply.

He looked up from under his brow, directly at Elin as if the guard wasn't there, startling him with moonlit-silver eyes. "I'm no threat to you. There was just a...misunderstanding with these other gentlemen earlier, and they don't quickly forget."

Elin found, thankfully, that he believed the man. "Let him go then. I can't get him cleaned up with his hands tied together."

The guard did so and then hesitated a moment, as if unsure what do to next. "Would you like me to come in there...with you?" The guards usually gave the men of the haram their privacy in the baths—it was their job to protect, not to ogle—but Jurah clearly didn't feel the same faith in the stranger's intentions that Elin did.

Elin looked again into the strange, pale eyes. Seeing no malice there, he said, "We'll be fine. You can watch the door to ensure a little privacy for our new guest, and I'll call out if I have any need of you."

Jurah looked uncertain, but released the man, clearly feeling himself on the subordinate end of the equation in this interaction.

Elin stepped forward and opened the door to the baths, gesturing for the man to follow. "It's just a bath, really," he said to the skeptical Jurah as he closed the door behind them.

THE BATHS WERE unlike anything Hathar had ever seen. Granted, it was a palace, so he had expected luxury, but not on this scale. Large enough to easily accommodate twenty men, the room was completely clad in glowing white marble interrupted only by tasteful, intricate mosaics of fanciful sea creatures. It was filled with warm, diffuse light from windows slatted for privacy and vast domes on the ceiling that seemed to be made of a thick, translucent glass.

Past an assortment of platforms and benches for preening and lounging, a steaming pool set into the floor took up a large corner of the room. Constantly refreshed by water bubbling forth from the mouths of carved stone fish that appeared to be eternally leaping from the walls above, the pool overflowed into discreet drains set around its edges.

As Hathar gawked at the opulent room, the young man who had taken him from the guard was preparing himself for the baths, removing his shirt and hanging it on one of a series of hooks carved into the stone near the door. Hathar looked back now, just in time to see him shucking off his loosely fitted silken trousers. This was another kind of opulence. The boy's beauty was at least the equal of the room. His form was slender, but not scrawny. His skin was smooth and full over the contours of his modest muscles, a testament to a life without lack and plenty of tender care. He was fair, but there was a golden undertone to his complexion that was echoed in the burnished gold of his curls and his uncanny amber eyes, which came into view as he straightened. Whoever ran this place had taste, Hathar had to give them that.

The now-naked man seemed to hesitate under Hathar's gaze before he gathered himself and said softly, "So. Uh...you'll need to take your clothes off before we get in. I'll have someone bring you something clean to wear once we're done."

"Of course." Hathar wasn't used to having an audience for this sort of thing, but he tried to act casual as he stripped. He wasn't smooth and sleek like the smaller man, but his sunbrowned skin and rugged muscles held their own appeal, and he hoped his companion might enjoy what he saw.

To his disappointment, the other man wasn't looking at him at all. He was instead busying himself collecting towels and implements from nearby shelves and carrying them over to a bench near the tub. Hathar wandered over and stretched a toe experimentally into the pool. It was extremely warm, and he pulled back a moment before easing one foot fully onto the first shallow step. As he was working his way slowly into the water, taking time to adjust to the heat, he was passed by the other man plunging unceremoniously into the depth of the pool, clearly unfazed by the temperature. He ducked his gold curls under the surface, came up sleek and gleaming, and then moved over to recline on an underwater bench against one wall.

"You might as well just soak for a while before we try to polish you up. It'll make it easier," he said lazily, with half-closed eyes.

Hathar made his way to another of the benches built into the tub and did his best to recline as carelessly as his companion had done. But the act of stretching backward tweaked the ribs that had been bruised in last night's tussle, and he grunted urgently and sat back up.

"Are you all right?" The other man looked over with sudden concern.

"Fine, fine. Just...a little sore from my meeting with the authorities last night."

"They injured you?"

"Well, to be fair, I injured them first. I was just minding my own business, and next thing I know, some wretch in a uniform is grabbing me. I may have reacted on instinct. Seems to have worked out okay though; at least, this is the nicest jail I've ever been in."

There was a soft snort from the other bench. "This isn't a jail. Don't you even know where you are?"

Hathar felt like he was being set up for some kind of punch line, but couldn't for the life of him figure out what it was going to be. "I mean, I know I'm in the palace of Minal'taneen..." he trailed off.

"You've got that much right, but more specifically, you're in the northeast wing, in the quarters of the thirty-sixth cohort of the haram of Her Eminence, The Dragon Shavanh Laab. Do me a favor and duck your head under the water so that your hair can soak for a bit."

"Wait." Prisons Hathar was used to, but his brain was reeling as he tried to come to terms with this new development. "Haram like...for sex?"

The other man gave a small sigh, the meaning of which was unclear. "And other things. But yes, for The Dragon's pleasure. She's a faithful servant of the god Helcamet, who delights in the erotic, so her acts are an offering of sorts.

"But really, I thought you must know all this. Why else would you be wandering around openly near the palace if you didn't mean to be spotted by a collector and brought here? Though you did try to fight them off, so I suppose I really don't know what you're about."

"I'm...not from around here," was Hathar's weak reply. "But why me anyway? How does walking around near the palace get me conscripted into a haram?"

"Well, you're *dahabi*, or at least the guards thought you were under all that muck. All *dahabi* men are property of The Dragon."

"*Dahabi*?" Hathar weighed the unfamiliar word on his tongue. "I'm sorry, I don't know what that means."

His companion was looking at him intently now, brow furrowed.

"It means...like me. Or, not like me, but close enough—with the yellow hair and the golden skin, and, well, I haven't seen eyes like yours before, but they're not brown like everyone else's, so I guess they're *dahabi*.

"Come on, let's wash your hair and see what color it is when it's not dulled with grime."

ELIN FELT ODD at first, grooming the other man. Surely he could do as much for himself. Then again, given the state of him, maybe he couldn't. Elin had vague memories of his own early days in the haram, when his only previous experience of a bath had been a brisk scrubbing with a coarse cloth and water heated on the fire.

"Let me know if I'm being too rough," he said, and set to working up a perfumed lather.

With a little soap, the man's hair was revealed to be more platinum than gold, and it ran straight and smooth through Elin's fingers. More than being new to the haram, he really was a foreign creature. He *had* said he wasn't from around here. That was of interest in itself, for though Minal'taneen sat on a pleasant enough harbor, no one came or went from it but the local fishermen, and steep mountains hemmed in the city on the landward side. There was a minor trade route through the mountains to the plains beyond, but the occasional travelers who came that way were all even darker of skin and eye than the people of the city.

"Do they have names where you come from?" Elin asked with half a smile as he carefully combed back the man's wet hair.

"Hathar," was the reply. "And the guard called you...Elin, was it?"

Elin nodded and reached for a washcloth.

"Sorry about that." Hathar chuckled. "I usually try to get introductions handled before the clothes come off, but nothing's really been going quite like usual since yesterday."

"Yes, well, I imagine you've got the right to be a little preoccupied under the circumstances. Really though, once you've settled in, you should find it quite pleasant here. The city guards were rough with you, but that doesn't happen inside the haram. The only violence you'll see is a little good-spirited wrestling between the men, if you're into that kind of sport. Other than that, for the price of occasional service to The Dragon, you can spend your days in luxury."

Elin dabbed gently around the wound on Hathar's brow bone, trying to clean it up without setting it bleeding again. The split itself was really quite small, and as the gore was cleared away, his charge started to look more like a treasured *dahabi* of the haram, and less like a disreputable brute.

"That's the hair and face done. You can probably handle everything else yourself. Take as long as you like, and then I'll help you with a shave."

"Oh?" There was a sly twinkle in Hathar's eyes. "But maybe I'd prefer it if you handled me. You give an excellent scalp massage. I'm sure I could use the same treatment all over, after being roughed up last night."

Elin knew what the other man was after. You didn't spend your life in an isolated community of healthy, idle young men without a thorough education in the kinds of things some of them got up to with one another in pursuit of pleasure. He had never really seen the appeal, to put it mildly, but something made him want to give Hathar what he was asking for anyway. Without any acknowledgment of the teasing glances cast his way, he lathered up a cloth and began to wash the rest of Hathar's body.

Much to his surprise, Elin found himself enjoying the act. He could feel Hathar's tension unwinding under his touch. The rippling contours of muscle, presumably the product of a life of hard work, were a fascinating contrast to his own slender body—the only one he had any occasion to touch under normal circumstances. Hathar relaxed against the wall of the pool, his eyes closed over that playful gleam, giving Elin full access to rub him down with gentle circular motions—not quite a massage, but more contact than was strictly needed to get clean.

Having worked from the shoulders down and the feet up, there was just one area left. Rubbing muscles was one thing, but that...

He handed the towel to Hathar. "Okay, now I *know* you can manage the last bit on your own. You finish up, and I'll get the shaving things ready." With his final words, he was already halfway up the steps, not leaving time for any cajoling.

HATHAR SIGHED TO himself, but figured he couldn't really be too disappointed, all considered. A full-body rubdown, *almost* anyway, from a beautiful boy in an opulent marble spa was a good sight better than at least fifty other realities he could imagine right now. Elin had had an effect, though, on that neglected part of Hathar's anatomy, and it seemed inappropriate to bring that to the other man's attention when he'd so clearly taken pains to avoid the matter. Hathar took a few minutes to meditate on concrete and completely un-alluring facts, willing his cock down to a more manageable state before stepping out of the pool to join Elin where he stood by a low stool near a mirror.

He had slung a towel around his waist for modesty, and Hathar did likewise, eyeing the collection of implements on the adjacent counter: a cup and brush; wooden tweezers; something like a straight razor, but rendered in a dark and glittering material; and a few bottles of what looked like oils and treatments for the skin.

"Help yourself," Elin said, gesturing to the shaving kit.

The brush and cup were standard enough. Hathar whipped up a foam and dabbed it onto his chin, obscuring several days' worth of coarse stubble. He then picked up the razor-like thing. On closer inspection, the blade seemed to be of dark glass, its edge shaped by careful chipping, leaving it murderously sharp but far less regular than any proper razor he'd ever attempted to shave with. Not to let something so simple get the better of him, he leaned close to the mirror and brought the blade to his face.

He puzzled over the proper angle for a minute before settling on an arrangement that would bring most of the blade flush against his skin, though the uneven edge meant that some of the high points dug in a little. As he was about to take his first stroke, he realized that Elin was watching him intently, with undisguised tension.

"What?"

"It' s just...you have shaved before, haven't you? You look like you're about to cut yourself to ribbons."

"Yes, I've shaved before! But what is this thing? Don't you have a real razor around? I don't know where to start when the blade's not even straight."

"That is a real razor. You don't use the whole blade at once like you're trying to cut your face off. Just use it delicately." Under Elin's gaze, Hathar made an uncertain attempt to adjust his grip to something more "delicate," but he must have failed since a moment later Elin said, "Maybe I should do that for now too, then. I can teach you later, but you've probably done enough bleeding for the time being. Have a seat."

Hathar handed over the blade without protest and settled himself on the stool. Elin approached with a thoughtful, concentrated expression, gently tipped Hathar's head to the side, and began carefully scraping away the stubble. Elin's attention to detail was minute, and he ended up extremely close to Hathar's face, carefully pulling his skin against the grain to bring the hairs to attention before scraping them off smooth.

This intimacy was reawakening the desire Hathar had tamped down not long before, and Elin's breath against his cheek as he leaned in to look for missed hairs did nothing to ease matters. The fingers of Elin's free hand were soft and sure, stroking along in the wake of the blade to check for smoothness and raising gooseflesh on Hathar's arms.

As Elin moved in front of Hathar to make a few final strokes on his chin, the towel around his waist caught on Hathar's knee and pulled free from where it had been tucked in. The towel fell to the floor, but Elin was too intent on his task to take much notice. He placed a thumb on Hathar's sensitive lower lip and pulled it up to access the last bit of stubble. That touch, combined with the view of a perfect, supple backside now displayed in the mirror, cracked the last bit of Hathar's resolve. Before he could think better of it, he reached out to run a hand up Elin's thigh and cup his balls tenderly in a large palm.

Elin practically flew away from him at the contact—

"—Shit!" Hathar knew immediately that he'd made a major miscalculation as Elin fetched up against the far wall, the razor now shattered on the floor.

"Sorry. I'm sorry!" Hathar scrambled to make amends, kicking himself for alienating the first person who'd been decent to him since his arrival at the palace, and in such short order. He raised his hands in front of his chest in a gesture of surrender and kept his distance. "That was stupid. I just...it's been a while, and my dick got the better of me there for a second. No harm done, right?"

Looking marginally calmer, Elin took a deep breath and, after a long blink said, "Right. No harm done. I'll send someone along with some fresh clothes for you."

And with that, he left the room, throwing a fresh towel around his waist as he went.

Chapter Two

ELIN WAS AS good as his word, and shortly after his abrupt departure from the baths, another guard—this one somewhat smaller and with a more deferential air than the man who had held him bound earlier—arrived with a fresh suit of clothes.

The style seemed a little outlandish to Hathar's eye: wide trousers of finely woven green silk that wrapped and tied at the waist to fit over a thin cotton shirt trimmed with coordinating silk at collar and cuffs. It was in keeping with what he'd seen everyone else wearing though, and he didn't seem to have much choice in the matter, so he took the clothes gratefully and put them on.

Bathed and dressed, he was led up a flight of stairs and through large double doors to a room where he was shocked to encounter at least a dozen Elins, all with the same golden curls and burnished faces, dressed in coordinating shades of green. They were lounging about the well-appointed room in twos and threes, some reading, others chatting or idly playing cards. No one looked up at his entrance.

Given a moment to process, Hathar realized that the resemblance to Elin was only superficial. Beyond their near-identical coloring, the men before him were of a variety of builds and attitudes, none of them truly holding a candle to the beauty of the boy he'd just driven from the baths.

The guard cleared his throat and got a few glances. He seemed to decide that was good enough, and announced, "This is...ah..." He looked sheepishly to Hathar and whispered, "I didn't get your name."

"Hathar," Hathar replied, loud enough for anyone who cared to hear. The room was now focused on him.

"Right!" the guard began again. "This is Hathar. He's being added to the thirty-sixth cohort at the pleasure of Her Eminence. I know you'll all go out of your way to make him feel welcome." Hathar thought he caught a few less than enthusiastic expressions.

"Larin, Marik, he'll be bedding with you since you have room." Two men who had been chatting in the corner exchanged a dark look at that.

The guard then turned to Hathar and said more quietly, "You'll hear a chime for meals. Dining room is through there"—he gestured to their left—"and beds are through that door to the right.

"You're free to do as you wish. Wander the gardens, make some friends... Stick to the other men in green. We don't encourage mingling between the cohorts. If you need something, just ask any of the guards. Enjoy!" He clapped Hathar on the shoulder and then departed back through the double door, leaving him standing alone in the glare of a dozen sets of uncanny amber eyes.

He shifted his weight and ran a hand up the back of his neck, uncertain what to do next, finally focusing on a basket of fruit resting on a small table. He hadn't eaten since the rough breakfast he'd been fed before being brought up to bathe, so a snack seemed like a good place to start.

Many of the fruits were unfamiliar, so he selected an orange and went to take a seat on the unoccupied end of a velvet divan. The man seated on the far end looked up from his book to raise a single, critical eyebrow at Hathar and then stood and moved off to an armchair by the window.

Hathar shrugged to himself and went to work on his orange. When he had it peeled and his mouth was stuffed with the first juicy segment, a broad-shouldered man with a heavy jaw called out from across the room, "Where did you come from, anyway?" his voice dripping with scorn and distaste.

"My mother's cunt! Or so they tell me," Hathar replied cheerfully, before dragging a sleeve across his face to wipe the juice from his chin.

This earned him a disapproving cluck for his vulgarity but had the desired effect of ending that line of questioning.

No one else addressed him directly, but he caught snippets of whispered conversations around the room including unfavorable observations on his hair, skin, accent, and probable parentage. Starting to suspect that the guard's suggestion to "make friends" might have been less sincere than it had originally seemed, Hathar decided to see if things were any less hostile outside.

He rose and let himself out onto the veranda, where he was struck by the vista of craggy mountains rising up almost directly beyond the garden wall.

As he descended the stairs, he took in a broad lawn running up to a grove of shade trees and ornamental plantings. Good-natured shouting drew his attention to a cluster of men congregated around a pair grappling in a ring marked out on the grass. They were all wearing green, so Hathar wandered over and added himself unobtrusively to the group.

The wrestling men were clearly following some agreed upon code of conduct, because Hathar saw them passing up obvious openings to win, if the goal had been to incapacitate the opponent at all costs. He leaned over to the man nearest him and asked, "So how exactly does this work?" gesturing to the match before them.

The man turned, clearly annoyed that anyone would be asking such a stupid question, but his annoyance turned to bafflement as he took in Hathar's unfamiliar appearance. Wide-eyed, he asked, "Are you—? Who are you?"

"Hathar." He offered the man his hand. "I'm new."

The man squinted now. "New? Well I suppose you must be." He ignored Hathar's hand and, instead, turned back to face the wrestlers as he moved close to Hathar's side so that he could be heard over the commotion without yelling. "I'm Salin. I'm currently the, uh..." he seemed to be counting on his fingers "...fifth-best wrestler in the cohort.

"That's Nikil and Kasan in the ring. They're third and fourth. You can see they're pretty evenly matched. This has been going on for a while now. Kasan used to be first, actually, back when we were all kids. He got big fast and was able to take advantage, but we all caught up in time, and now he's struggling just to keep his place. Kiran's the one to beat now, but he's not here. This is just a little practice match."

Just then, one of the men in the ring managed to get the other pinned with an arm behind his back, and the onlookers cheered.

Salin returned to his lecture as another pair of men stripped off their shirts and moved into the ring. He gave Hathar a history of the major wins, losses, and upsets of the last decade followed by an overview of the rules, and was embarking on a discussion of the finer points of strategy when Hathar thought he caught a flash of someone of Elin's height and build moving among the trees on the far side of the lawn.

"Excuse me." He cut Salin off. "I'd love to hear more about this later, but I think I see my friend over there." Hathar headed off into the wooded area of the garden without waiting for a reply.

He followed the path he thought the maybe-Elin would have taken for a few yards. Not seeing anyone, he stopped to listen for a moment before a rustle of movement sent him pressing further into the trees. There was still no sign of Elin, but as he neared the garden wall, the sound was revealed to be that of a small stone fountain. Water streamed from the erect member of a stone man in the throes of ecstasy as he perpetually came into the mouth of a buxom stone woman who gazed up at him, the water overflowing to collect in a basin below. *Delights in the erotic indeed,* Hathar thought. *Pornographic, more like.*

The garden art had clearly been chosen by someone other than whoever had designed the scrupulously tasteful baths.

Hathar took one last look around and decided that, if Elin wasn't to be found, a little solitude might be better than any of his other options at the moment. He stretched himself on the warm stone ledge next to the water and let his mind relax into the play of light on the ripples.

FROM THE BUSHES just beyond, Elin watched. He hadn't been sure what to do with himself after leaving the baths. He'd felt strange. Unsettled. There was a rootless sense of urgency growing in him and no clear way to satisfy it.

He'd dressed, hoping to will his body back to normalcy with the cool reassurance of fresh silk, but when the clothes did nothing for his state of mind, he'd headed outside for some air and space.

There was a reason he wasn't one of the more favored men of the haram. It wasn't his looks, which he knew to be at least the equal of anyone else in his cohort; it was his disinclination to...perform.

Years ago, when the boys of the thirty-sixth cohort were beginning to blossom into men, they were taken off by ones and twos in the evening, carefully bathed and dressed for an audience with The Dragon. They would return in the morning, some looking rather dazed and worse for wear, others vibrating with barely contained excitement. Invariably, lusty bragging would commence of unmentionable acts heretofore unimagined played out between the young men and the beautiful dragon queen. The unquestioned opinion in the wing was that it was a very fine and fortunate thing to be called up to The Dragon's service.

Elin, however, could not quite manage to echo this seemingly universal excitement. He'd only ever seen The Dragon in passing—at the head table on feast days, or when she came whisking imperiously through the wing on her extremely occasional inspections. Why would he suddenly want to touch her, especially in the intimate ways the other boys described, or worse yet, have her touch him? There was talk of mouths on mouths, mouths on...other things. His stomach churned at the notion that he might be forced to do those things, and he hoped against hope that he might somehow manage to go unnoticed indefinitely.

Of course, that was unlikely in a cohort of only twenty, and in due time, his turn came. He was called up with another boy named Larin.

Larin had been to see The Dragon once before, and could barely contain his glee at being summoned again. He babbled all through their preparations, regaling Elin with exaggerated retellings of his last encounter and bawdy imaginings of what this evening might hold. This only served to deepen Elin's sense of dread, but at least did him the favor of filling what would otherwise have been an extremely nervous silence.

At last, they were shown into The Dragon's private chambers, where she awaited them wearing an inviting smile, a dressing gown of translucent silk chiffon that mimicked and reflected the flickers of the candle flames, and nothing else.

As the door clicked discreetly closed behind them, she beckoned the boys over to the bed. Larin's earlier bravado had diminished, but he still trotted over eagerly at her invitation and took a seat next to her on the gleaming coverlet. Elin took a few token steps in their direction, but hung back and watched with growing horror as she began to pet and fondle his companion.

"So nice to see you again," she murmured as she ran her fingers through Larin's hair, stroking down over his neck and throat to his chest, where she gave an appreciative squeeze to one of his pectoral muscles. "You've been training hard, I see. Very nice. I like my boys to take care of themselves."

She slid her hand further down, teasing at the bulge in Larin's trousers as she leaned in for a slow and penetrating kiss.

After a few moments she withdrew, leaving Larin glassy-eyed and gaping, and turned her attention to Elin.

"And what about you, little one? I don't think I've had the honor of your presence in my chambers before. Come closer." She held out her hands.

Elin willed himself forward as every fiber of his being screamed to bolt for the door. He knew this was his duty—the fair price to pay for the luxury he lived in and the fate he was born to. *Dahabi* men belonged to The Dragon. This was essentially what he was *for*, and so he stepped closer, placing his trembling hands in hers.

"You don't need to be afraid," she purred. "Come, look at me."

He realized he was staring at the rug and pried his gaze up to meet hers. She really was beautiful. Her large eyes, framed by delicately arching brows, were a dark brown that mostly concealed the reptilian slitted shape of her pupils. Chestnut waves fell around her shoulders, and her lips were full and moist from the kiss she'd shared with Larin. Even so, Elin's admiration for her was purely aesthetic, as if she were a fine work of art. He couldn't summon any feeling but revulsion for what he was certain would be coming next.

Still maintaining her grasp, she stood from the bed and pulled him closer, sliding his hands in and around her waist, under her gown. His heart began to pound and his head to swim at the touch of her bare flesh, the panic rising in his throat.

"See? It's nice. Touch. Feel..."

He wasn't soothed by her gentle tone. Instead, as she guided his hands to her ample breasts, his fear and distaste reached a crescendo. There was an insistent low pounding in his ears, and before he knew what was happening, he had vomited all down the front of her glorious robe.

She released him then, leaping back in horror, and summoned the guards to take the boys away and a maid to change and bathe her.

He had not been called to The Dragon's service again.

Since then, Elin had come to believe there was a fundamental difference between himself and the other men. Sure, they varied in the degree to which they reveled in their service to The Dragon, but they all seemed at least able to do it. Many of them made use of one another as well, filling their time with the same carnal games they'd learned in The Dragon's chambers, though played with slightly different equipment. Elin, meanwhile, was completely outside these interactions, unable to fathom the appeal.

He did sometimes bring himself off alone, in the baths, but when he did so it was more a mechanical impulse than an act of passion. He didn't entertain fantasies of a lover or of any acts that might involve another, only the uncomplicated pleasure followed by release, more a massage than an act of hedonism.

This all being the case, it had come as a surprise when he found himself feeling tenderness at the look in the newcomer's eyes when he first assured Elin he meant no malice as they stood outside the baths. He told himself in the moment that it was just sympathy born of memories of his own first days in the haram, but there was something in that moment of contact that left Elin feeling as if they already knew one another. When the man spoke of his injuries at the hands of the guards, he had felt a real pang of protective alarm.

Agreeing to bathe Hathar, in the light of that lascivious, teasing gleam, had been an unprecedented act. Elin's mind returned again and again to the feel of those ropy muscles unwinding under the washcloth.

Still, that contact was all arguably innocent.

The moment that was causing Elin to question everything was what had happened next. Hathar had touched him, intimately, and he had reacted on pure instinct as he would to any touch of that kind: fleeing, heart racing. But beneath the panic, there was something else—foreign as it was, a hint of desire.

That was the crux of it. There was a part of Elin that wished he'd stayed there and explored the possibilities of Hathar's touch.

That part was at odds with the rest of Elin, which had sent him fleeing into the shrubbery at the east end of the garden as soon as he caught sight of Hathar standing near the wrestlers on the lawn. There was too much to process to be able face him right now. What would he say? What *could* he say?

So here he sat, shielded from view by a stand of ferns but able to make out most of Hathar where he lay on the fountain's edge, afraid to leave in case the rustling of branches might give him away.

He allowed his mind to wander. What if he hadn't fled from Hathar's advance? What if he'd leaned into the caress of that calloused palm and tangled his fingers in the damp, silken strands of his hair? They were so close; they might have kissed.

Elin imagined the sensation of his lips on Hathar's, warm and yielding, or maybe eager and intense, his freshly shaven chin cool in contrast. The thought of their tongues meeting sent a shocking rush of blood to his groin that caused him to gasp softly and sigh as it was followed by a tingling wave of goose bumps.

What might it be like to be held by Hathar? To rest his head on that sturdy chest, to be close enough to listen to his beating heart while those same arms he'd massaged earlier today encircled him with strength. He stole a glance through the ferns at Hathar's broad shoulders, barely obscured by his thin cotton shirt, and in his imaginings his hands roamed up to grasp them, to explore and appreciate each swell and valley.

In reality, Elin's hand went tentatively to his flushed member, which surprised him with its rigidity. His erections tended to come in the mornings, as simple biological necessity, but this was something very different. Daydream Hathar murmured tenderly into his ear, and he could feel himself swell in response. He closed his eyes, breathed deeply, and began to stroke.

His visions became more fragmented: strong hands, affectionate looks, the whisper of breath across his skin. His pleasure built as he gave himself over to the fantasy that this stranger was very much not a stranger, that the familiarity he felt was reciprocated and amplified and was being expressed through sweet sensation. His own hand was now Hathar's, bringing him swiftly and assuredly to climax. He let out a choked yelp as he came, stunned to find the moment almost over before he knew it was upon him.

Elin's heart thudded in the ensuing silence, and he willed it to be quiet, watching anxiously for any indication that he had been heard, ready to run, for all the good it would do him. It seemed, though, that Hathar had fallen asleep, as soft snores carried on the breeze.

Thanking his lucky stars, Elin stood as quietly as he could, wiped his hand on the hem of his shirt, and made a cursory attempt to tidy himself up, flicking bits of leaf litter from his trousers. He crept away from the fountain, and Hathar, and the whole mess, completely unsure what to do next.

Chapter Three

IT WAS A delightful afternoon two days later, and Elin was lying beneath a tree, letting his thoughts wander as he admired the play of sunlight through the gently swaying leaves.

Without warning, someone threw himself to the ground nearby, sending a dull thud through the carefully maintained sod. Elin glanced over and was greeted by a sweep of silvery hair and the distinctive profile of Hathar's faintly hawkish nose as he also stared blankly up at the canopy, his arms crossed over his head.

They hadn't spoken since Elin walked out of the bath so abruptly. In fact, he'd been carefully avoiding Hathar, afraid of an awkward confrontation and still wrestling with his own muddled feelings about what had happened between them. And he wasn't sure what was appropriate to do now. He couldn't very well get up and walk away without being obviously rude, which wasn't exactly what he wanted, but he couldn't really think of anything to say either. It seemed safest to pretend obliviousness and hope for the best.

The silence lasted only a matter of seconds.

"Can I ask you something? I mean, after the other day and all…"

When Hathar trailed off, waiting, Elin responded, uncertainly, "I guess."

"How do you stand these guys?"

Elin snorted. He didn't know how to reply to that. It had never occurred to him that there was anything to "stand" exactly. The men he lived with were as much a fixture in his life as the walls of the palace. They were there, always with him and around him, so inescapable as to hardly merit thought.

Apparently no response was required because Hathar went on: "They act like I'm diseased. Every time I start to talk, they look at me like I've grown a second head, but then, when *they* talk it's this endless blah blah blah about who beat who at wrestling and who The Dragon favors most, and I start wanting to crack heads together. But I *don't*, because I'm trying to be *polite*, fat lot of good that's done me. Do you know they've got me sleeping on the floor?"

In fact, that morning, Elin had noticed Hathar rising from a pile of spare quilts tucked into an alcove by the bedchamber door, but he'd assumed the exile was voluntary.

"I was assigned to a bed with Mary and Larry, or whatever their names are, but they told me I had to be in the middle and then made sure there *was* no middle. They kept throwing knees and elbows in my way until I gave up and left."

"You mean Marik and Larin," Elin volunteered.

"I probably do, but they call me Hithrik, so I guess we're even."

Elin had to laugh a little to hear the big man so peevish over petty slights.

"They're afraid of you, of course," Elin said, as the power dynamic among the men presented itself as a vague network in his mind.

"Marik and Larin are The Dragon's favorites from our cohort. Everyone else has three to a bed, but they haven't had to share since Kenik was expelled after he tried to murder Rian for replacing him in Salin's affections. They wouldn't be happy to give up that privilege under any circumstances, but then you, you're..." He wasn't sure he wanted to say out loud all the things that Hathar was. "You're different than the rest of us. It's easy to imagine The Dragon might prize you more highly. Of course, it's also possible she won't like you at all. I mean, she does seem to have a type." A pack of four haram men, all with hair and skin in slightly varying tones of darkish gold walked past as if to illustrate the point.

"So then, from there, the fear would all trickle down," Elin continued. "First you steal Marik and Larin's bed. Next thing you know, The Dragon's not calling them up as much anymore. The slightly less-favored men see her even less, and at the bottom of the pile, maybe one or two more end up as neglected errand boys like me. The way they see it, you can't mean anything but trouble for everyone.

"Although if they had a little more foresight, they'd be sucking up instead of making things hard on you. That is, if it *is* true that they imagine you're such a terrible threat. Or maybe they hope they can make you so uncomfortable that you won't be able to perform for The Dragon when the time comes, and then they won't have to worry about you anymore at all." He paused.

"You're not wrong though. They really are boring to talk to, even when they're not afraid of you."

That got a laugh from Hathar, a rich, warming sound that seemed to vibrate through the earth where they lay.

Hathar propped himself up on an elbow. "Can't I just opt out of the whole Dragon thing? Lizard ladies really aren't my style anyway. I'm happy to lie low and let the others have their fun."

"Sorry," Elin replied, "but it's not that easy. She'll send for you when she wants you, and the more she likes you, the more she'll send for you."

"But she doesn't like you? That seems a little hard to believe."

Elin glanced over again, this time to see that unnerving silver twinkle focused squarely on him, and blushed. "Well...no. You may have noticed I don't really have a natural aptitude for the types of activities she most values."

"Oh, I don't know about that. You seem clever enough. Surely you could make up for inborn talent with some careful study."

The flirtatious tone in Hathar's last words was unmistakable, and Elin lapsed back into contemplation, letting his mind expand as he focused once more on the shifting light.

Silence settled between them for several minutes as Elin floated in a sea of possibilities, twinges of curiosity, fear, revulsion, and desire rearing up out of the murk at the twists and turns of the hypothetical. He was conscious of Hathar's presence nearby, as if their energies were touching even though their bodies lay several feet apart, and it was not an unwelcome sensation.

"Sorry to come over here and unload on you like that," Hathar said at last. "What were you doing before I showed up, anyway?"

"Just watching the leaves," Elin replied lamely, fully expecting to be met with ridicule.

"They're nice, aren't they?" he got instead. "The way the different layers make some shine almost gold, while others are dark and deep green, and then sometimes the sun peeks through and flashes when the wind catches them...

"It reminds me of the play of light on the sea. I could stand on deck and watch the waves for hours, seems like, letting my mind go where it wanted. It's always the same but always changing, and somehow, getting lost in that lets me turn off the wiseass part of my brain and get some real thinking done sometimes."

"You've been on the sea?" Elin asked curiously.

"Spent most of my life there, at this point. Highly recommended. You've got comforts here, that's for sure, but there's a different kind of luxury in the freedom to go wherever the wind takes you."

"Oh."

It somehow hadn't occurred to Elin that Hathar might have a life outside the palace he would wish to return to. He'd been raised to believe that what they had in the haram was the best of all possible worlds.

"Will you miss it?" he asked

Hathar chuckled. "Well, I hope I won't be missing it too long."

Before Elin could corral his thoughts to question Hathar further, a crystal chime rang out, calling them in for the evening meal.

Hathar was already on his feet and headed back toward the residence as he called over his shoulder, "Soup's on!" and gestured for Elin to keep up.

IN THE DARK of the night, Elin was returning stealthily to the bedchamber after relieving himself. The palace was silent, and it seemed everyone was asleep.

As he entered, he passed the alcove where Hathar slept in exile.

The powerful, sun-browned man had pushed aside most of his blankets, and lay sprawled with his hands thrown casually over his head and one leg protruding into the hall. Moonlight shone in from a high window on the opposite side of the room, setting his hair aglow and picking out the contours of his muscles in stark shadow.

Standing here, gazing down at him, Elin was aware of that same warm connection he'd noticed earlier under the trees when without physically touching, their consciousnesses seemed to already be in communion. Without the pressure of Hathar's expectant gaze, Elin could finally confess to himself that he would like to touch him with more than just his mind. He imagined joining him there in the pile of soft duvets, allowing his hands to travel over the fascinating planes and textures of that beautiful body, this time without a towel, without the cover of water, and without the pretense of innocent intent.

As he looked on, lost in thought, Hathar's eyes suddenly shot open. The corner of his mouth quirked up, and he whispered, "Are you plotting to kill me, or fuck me?"

A jolt of shock and embarrassment seared through Elin. He turned to leave, but Hathar reached out to grab his ankle.

"Come back," he said, just loud enough for Elin to hear. "I don't really think you're trying to kill me."

"I just..." Elin knelt to close the distance between them and keep his voice as low as possible.

His earlier desire to touch Hathar hadn't been squelched by the shock, only set back a bit, and now, so close, it roared forth with a vengeance. Bleary with sleep and careless with desire, he blurted, "I just really wanted to touch you."

"Then touch." Hathar smiled and stretched invitingly.

Elin reached out, simultaneously thrilled and horrified at what he was about to do. He placed a tentative hand on Hathar's chest, experimentally stroking the moonlit curls he found there. Working downward, he played his fingers over the subtle hills of Hathar's ribs and onto the softer yielding skin of his flank, which brought a quiet moan of encouragement. He tried that spot again and heard Hathar's breath catch.

Gaining confidence, he began to explore with both hands, keeping his attention on his torso at first before branching out to caress Hathar's throat and run his fingers up the back of his neck and into that impossibly smooth hair. He twisted it around his fingers, reveling in the texture, and pulled with just the slightest pressure, causing Hathar to arch and smile in response. His eyes were dilated with pleasure, more inky pools than silver moons now, but with no less sparkle as he gazed up at Elin.

"May I touch you as well?" he asked huskily.

Elin paused, unsure how to explain without ruining the moment all the thoughts and fears warring in his mind. He'd been haunted by the memory of Hathar's brief touch and craved another taste, but just that, a taste, not too much more. At least...probably. For now. A man like Hathar might have little patience for his tentatively unfolding libido. He feared things going faster and further than he desired. At the same time though, he feared almost as strongly things going nowhere at all.

Summoning his nerve, Elin took one of Hathar's large hands and brought it to his cheek, doing his best to suppress the urge to tremble. He held it there a moment, nuzzling into the cup of Hathar's palm and relishing the warm tingle that grew and spread from the point of contact, raising goose bumps on his skin. Elin guided the hand down to his chest and surprised himself with the jolt of pleasure that seized him when Hathar's fingers grazed his nipple. He lingered there, encouraging Hathar to stroke the tight brown nub, but not releasing his hand. Finally, he skimmed Hathar's hand down over his stomach, onto his thigh, and down to his bent knee. He circled the kneecap and came back up, angling this time toward his sensitive inner thigh. Elin slowed the pace as their hands crept ever higher. He was growing nervous again, but the flush of pleasure that grew more persistent the closer they came to his groin strengthened his resolve.

He played that edge for a while, tracing their hands up to the crease of his thigh and then back down, not yet quite ready to take that last, bold step.

Finally, Hathar whispered, "Why don't you come down here and lay with me? We can touch with more than just hands."

Having gotten this taste, the drive for more contact was high, and Elin didn't need to be asked twice. He released Hathar's hand and dove under the blankets, snugly aligning their bodies, his head on Hathar's shoulder and an arm thrown over his chest, their legs tangled below.

The sensation of so much warm, naked skin against his own was dizzying and sent a surge to Elin's crotch. Beyond that though, in such close proximity, the connection he'd begun to notice with Hathar seemed amplified. He felt tenderly toward the other man, and hoped the tenderness being reflected back on him wasn't imagined. Surely Hathar's actions this night weren't that of a man only after physical pleasures.

Elin squeezed Hathar where he held him, nuzzling his face into the crook of his neck and inhaling deeply of his scent before he dared to plant a small kiss there. This gesture was met by a blissful murmur from Hathar, who turned slightly and placed a similar kiss on Elin's hair.

Emboldened by this demonstration of affection and wishing to in some way repay Hathar for the patience he'd shown thus far, Elin ran a hand back down his furred chest and over the taut and rippling stomach to the nest of sandy curls beyond. He stroked the hair for a moment before taking a hesitant grasp of Hathar's semi-erect cock. At that touch, he felt Hathar's demeanor change from a relaxed, basking pleasure to something more focused. Hathar brought an arm up around Elin's shoulders in a possessive grasp, and his breathing became faster and shallower.

Elin firmed his grip and gave a few experimental strokes. The rod stiffened gratifyingly in his hand as the silky skin slid up and down the shaft. Soon, on an upstroke, he encountered a small amount of fluid, which he caught up with his fingers and smoothed over the head, sliding Hathar's foreskin gently back.

Hathar moaned his appreciation of that maneuver and used the arm around Elin's shoulders to hoist him up slightly, bringing their faces into closer alignment. Hathar kissed, gently at first, at Elin's temple, and cheek, and the corner of his mouth. Hesitation quickly diminishing, Elin met him there, kissing him full on the lips, his blood heating at the warm, moist contact. Soon, Hathar's tongue was teasing at his closed mouth, seeking entrance. It met little resistance, and Elin's arousal redoubled at this unprecedented intimacy. He ground his rigid cock against Hathar's hip and picked up the pace of his stroking.

The kiss became urgent, Hathar's lips bearing down hard on Elin's their tongues probing and tangling. Hathar groaned and lifted his pelvis, urging Elin on. Elin's grip on Hathar tightened, and as he reached the end of a stroke, he gave a slight twist over the slick head of Hathar's cock with the loose skin collected there. This had more than the desired result, and Hathar just barely choked back a cry that would have certainly roused the room. With a few repetitions of the action, Hathar abruptly released Elin's mouth and arched up off the floor, his head craning back and his face contorting as his spend splattered thickly over his stomach.

Elin pulled back a bit, in awe of what he'd done. This rugged, beautiful man from beyond the palace had come undone and lay now in a disheveled heap because of his touch. His thoughts were a jumble as he tried to sort out what this might mean and what might come next. With the slightest hint of the old panic surfacing at this new uncertainty, Elin quickly sat up and wiped his sticky palm on the corner of some cast-off bedding. He did the same for the worst of the mess on Hathar's belly. When Hathar gave him a heavy-lidded glance, Elin smiled back quickly, scrambled to his feet, and made a beeline for his own bed. He thought he heard a soft, "Hey," from the alcove as he departed, but he didn't look back, and instead wedged himself awkwardly into his middle position between Rian and Nikil, trying not to wake them.

Elin's own erection was still asserting itself, but he was in no hurry to tamp it down. Each time his arousal started to flag, he would revisit the moment of Hathar's climax or the passionate kisses just before, and be painfully hard once again. He held onto that feeling of intense connection, turning it over in his mind, his heart and cock warm until he drifted off to sleep, buoyed by dreams of platinum hair and silver eyes.

Chapter Four

HATHAR HAD NO idea what to make of this beguiling golden boy. He was shy and inexperienced, that much was clear, but he seemed drawn to Hathar in the same unnameable way that Hathar was drawn to him—a novel sensation that Hathar wanted to explore very, very fully.

He considered himself a seasoned man of the world. Seafaring adventurers were supposed to do their share of bawdy bedding, racking up a store of tales to tell over a pint and a few willing partners in every port. He had told himself, admiring that golden backside and flirting his way to an intimate rubdown in the steamy comfort of the baths, that this would be just another such interlude—a barely believable story he'd probably embellish beyond all credulity in the retelling, good enough to win him at least a round at the bar, if not two.

If he was being honest though, there had been a glimmer of what was to come in those first moments of their acquaintance. When Elin had confidently sent the guard away, entrusting himself to an unknown brute based on nothing but his word and a flash of eye contact, Hathar had sensed the first hint of sympathetic feeling. When he had so stupidly made his ham-fisted move and sent Elin running from him, he had a real pang of regret and worry—not for his own diminished chance of conquest, but for the damage done to that faintly glimmering link developing between them.

Given what had happened up to that point, the events of last night seemed a near-miraculous development. It might almost have been a dream, but he woke with concrete evidence in the form of a blanket stiffened with his spend, corroborated by Elin's renewed avoidance of his gaze.

That stung. Hathar was nearly certain he hadn't done anything wrong this time. He'd allowed Elin to guide his hand, not moving to do a thing that wasn't invited. He'd been pleasantly shocked by Elin's boldness in getting him off, and intensely aroused by the trust displayed. When Elin had left abruptly, without coming himself, Hathar was sorry. He'd been looking forward to returning the favor, and possibly even holding that smooth and slender body warm against him for the rest of the night. Elin had smiled as he went, though, and given no indication of a problem that would lead him to avoid Hathar in the morning.

Perhaps he was imagining avoidance where there was only distraction. Last night had given them both something to think about. He pledged to give it at least until the afternoon to see if Elin would come around first, and, if not, to seek him out for explanation. That would work well anyway, because it was already his fifth day in Minal'taneen, and he had some other business to attend to if he wasn't going to muck things up for his crew more royally than he already had.

HATHAR HAD USED his time in the palace so far to familiarize himself with the upper level of the northeast wing, where he and the rest of the thirty-sixth cohort were sequestered. The layout was basic:

a bedchamber, a dayroom, and a dining hall, laid out one after another down the length of the wing. They were on the backside of the palace, practically tucked into the mountains, with no view of the harbor that he knew was due west. There was a broad veranda off the dayroom, from which he could observe the rest of the back of the palace. The bulk of the building, which he assumed held the more public areas, was a long rectangle stretching north to south, and at the distant end he could see another wing that mirrored the one he was in, angling off at a diagonal to the southeast. He knew, from his observations before he was captured, that matching wings also protruded from the front of the building to the north and southwest, angled to take in a view of the sea.

Stairs led from the veranda to the gardens below, which were divided by hedges and ornamental stones into discrete paddocks adjoining each of the residential wings. He could catch occasional glimpses of men from the thirty-fourth and thirty-seventh cohorts in their silks of violet and blue from his vantage point. The men were free to come and go as they wished, but it was only a nominal freedom, since a great wall arced from wing to wing, fifteen feet tall and stuccoed smooth to discourage any thoughts of climbing. Even if one of the haram men were capable of scaling the featureless face, he would have to confront the guards who waited at the top. They strolled casually there, with no apparent malice, as if simply taking in the view, but Hathar's earlier encounter with their brethren had shown that appearances could be deceiving.

From the windows on the other side of the dayroom and dining hall, he could see the back half of the northwest wing, as expected. The palace was essentially cradled in a triangular valley, widening toward the sea, and from this vantage point it was apparent how the massive walls were married to the ancient mountain stone. It rose up at the extremity of the building, the lower floor lost in the native crags, the upper story just barely rising above.

There was a large double door off the dayroom that led into a foyer of sorts with a hall leading off to the western wing and a stairwell to the lower stories and the shared baths. He'd come through there on the first day and not given a lot of thought to the area, since two guards stood on constant watch just beyond the doors.

There was another less obvious—and so possibly more interesting—exit from their quarters. Meals, of course, had to be delivered from somewhere, and the staff who discreetly cleaned up after the men and saw to their needs needed a less ostentatious way to come and go. Narrow doors were set into the walls of both the dayroom and dining room that seemed to get much less attention than the grand entrance, and he hoped these might offer him some hope for unhindered exploration.

Beyond these observations, Hathar hadn't had much time to go in search of his prize. His first day had been a blur of lust and introductions, and then he had wasted time on trying to befriend someone, anyone, who might be willing and able to tell him something useful. He had allowed himself to get a little caught up in other matters, but today, he hoped to make real progress toward his ultimate goal.

OVER BREAKFAST, HE started with the gambit that seemed most obvious.

Hathar waved over one of the omnipresent guards and said, "So, if I'd like to get a little gold and go into town, how do I arrange that?"

The guard looked at him a moment, clearly perplexed.

"Gold?"

"Yes...? Or the customary coin of the land. I was just hoping to pick up a few necessities."

"Oh!" The guard seemed relieved. "You don't."

Well, it was a given that obvious gambits might not be the surest path to success.

"No?"

"Oh no, anything you need, just let one of us know and we'll see to it that you're taken care of. No need to leave the palace at all."

No need. Right. Just lie back and fuck The Dragon and grow old in the lap of luxury, until you die without the inconvenience of experiencing a day of real life.

He forced a smile and said, "Ah, well, how wonderfully convenient. Thank you then. I'll compose a list when I have a few minutes, I suppose."

The guard nodded obligingly and returned to his post.

On to plan B then.

With breakfast finished, washed and changed and ready to face the day, Hathar headed to the large double doors in the dayroom. He stepped through, trying to appear casual but braced for a heavy blow or a restraining grab from the men who stood on the other side.

Nothing happened.

Hathar walked through like a free man and headed to a second set of double doors that divided the foyer from the greater palace beyond. There too he passed without incident, emerging into a large gallery lined with marvelously lifelike paintings depicting scandalous scenes, some of which even his most stalwart seamen would blush to describe. Clearly, the same visionary who'd outfitted the gardens had had a hand in the art as well. He couldn't help but notice that all the men were depicted with tight golden curls and fair skin with that same distinctive undertone, and wondered with a faint flare of protectiveness whether Elin had ever been pressed into service as a model.

The gallery was thickly carpeted, muffling footsteps and stifling echoes, but as he moved on past the paintings, Hathar became aware of a soft but persistent padding behind him. He turned to see one of the guards from the door at a discreet distance seemingly lost in contemplation of a particularly sordid scene being played out between a dark haired woman and no less than five of the ubiquitous golden boys.

Hathar pressed on, curious to see how this might play out. If he was honest, he wasn't really sure what he was looking for anyway, so he might as well bring some company along.

To the end of the gallery, through a series of salons and reception rooms that lined the back of the upper floor, down the grand stairway to the hall below, the guard maintained his unobtrusive pursuit.

Hathar briefly entertained the idea of continuing his walk right out the front door. He was reasonably certain he could take the man shadowing him in hand-to-hand combat, if it came to that. He didn't seem to be armed with anything more than size or muscle.

The sight, through a window, of twenty more guards arrayed outside put an end to that line of thought.

Instead, Hathar wandered the lower level, taking himself on a tour through a grand formal dining room, a ballroom, and a small chapel. He ended up at a dead end in an impressive throne room, dominated by a single massive seat of dark and richly worked wood. Velvet curtains hung behind the throne, and with a prickle of hopeful curiosity, Hathar swept them aside to peek behind.

A narrow passageway led off to the left behind the curtains, and without a second thought, Hathar ducked through it. He emerged into a disappointingly ordinary dressing room, probably used before The Dragon's formal public appearances. There was a table and mirror, an armchair, and an empty rack for hanging clothes. A few boxes and bottles were on the table, but not so much as a brooch or comb of interest or value. Before he had fully taken stock of the room, the guard rushed in behind him, finally closing the gap he'd carefully maintained between them.

"Can I, uh…help you find something?" The guard seemed almost embarrassed to be confronting a man of the haram.

Hathar looked around. "Well, I was really just taking myself on a tour of the place. Astonishing architecture, eh? Of course, I've never been inside anything grander than a really nice barn before this week, so what do I know?" He laughed, and the guard relaxed perceptibly.

"Since you're here though, I was wondering if there was some kind of library perhaps? I thought there might be some maps, or a history of the palace's construction, or something like that."

"Oh, of course! This way."

He followed the guard back the way they'd come and into a surprisingly small room on the other side of the chapel. Hathar had expected something a little more impressive as the library of such a grand palace, but maybe The Dragon wasn't much of a reader. There was a desk in the middle of the room and a couple of upholstered chairs by the window. The walls were lined with shelves, but the books on the shelves were widely spaced and seemed to have been chosen and laid out more for aesthetic purposes rather than easy reference.

Still, the guard was able to find what he was looking for and went directly to a shelf over one of the chairs to take down a slim volume and a stack of papers.

"So this," he said, gesturing to the book, "is a history of Minal'taneen, including a bit on the palace, and then here"–he slid the papers across the desk—"is a map. The different floors are laid out on different pages so that you can see how they fit together.

"Thank you." Hathar gave the man a cordial smile and waited for him to excuse himself, but he made no move to go.

"I'll just..." He gestured vaguely and took a seat at the desk, the guard continuing to hover just behind his shoulder.

Attempting to ignore the sensation of eyes on the back of his neck, Hathar picked up the book first. It was extremely small for something purporting to be a history of a centuries-old kingdom, and a glance through the pages explained why. It was, essentially, a child's primer, barely glossing over the high points of The Dragon's reign in glib and glowing terms, heavily illustrated with simple woodcuts.

The Dragon came to our land a long, long time ago to keep us safe.

Here, a winged serpent soared over a city on one page, and a woman stood with hands outstretched and a benevolent smile on the next.

Her palace on the hill is made of stone and has many rooms. She hosts great feasts there.

This illustration stretched across both pages and was clearly meant to be a simplified image of the palace.

She treasures her dahabi. They live in the palace too.

A collection of men lounged around the same woman from the first page, casting adoring looks up at her.

Hathar flipped through the remaining pages. It just went on like that. The Dragon was good and kind and took care of the people of Minal'taneen from her beautiful palace and they should all be thankful and sing hey nonny nonny. He set it aside and went on to the maps.

They were marginally more interesting and at least intended for adult consumption it seemed, but so edited, whether to make things more clear or prevent secrets from being discovered, as to be useless. He could pick out almost all the rooms he had seen, but details like the dressing chamber behind the throne room and the passages that he knew had to lay behind the unobtrusive doors back in the northeast wing were omitted. He was able to confirm that the southern wings were residential just like the northern ones, which he had already suspected. He could also retrace the route he had followed when he first arrived: down some exterior stairs cut into the stone through a side door into the basement, and then to an area marked "storage" on the map, which he knew to be more like a modest dungeon. He'd been made to sleep there, bound, the first night and then walked up to the baths by a back stair, which was also not pictured. Things had been a little chaotic when he was brought in, so it was good to confirm the layout, but there was nothing shown that he couldn't have guessed.

Realizing with a sigh that there was nothing more he was going to learn from the materials provided, he stood, almost knocking over the guard as he slid the chair back.

"So there's nothing else?" Hathar looked around at the books again, but they all seemed to be either low-level educational texts, or novels.

"Well..." The guard glanced around as well. "I'm told there are some really good romances! But nothing more about the palace or the kingdom, if that's what you're looking for."

"Sure. I'll take a romance. Whatever you recommend. Can I take it back to my quarters?"

The guard, who had turned to look more closely at the titles on the shelves, seemed to find what he was looking for. He slid it out and turned back to Hathar. "The men are always asking for this one, so it should be good. And of course you can take it back with you. Just give it to any of the staff when you're done, and they'll bring it back here. In fact, you don't need to come down here at all. When you want another book, just send someone."

"Oh, of course!" Hathar's teeth were grinding, but he tried to summon a cheery smile. "Why would I even want to leave our wing? I'm just not used to such service."

"Of course, of course! Happy to help. Shall we?" The guard handed over the book and gestured for Hathar to leave first.

They walked back to the northeast wing with no further pretense of coincidental following. Hathar now felt clearly escorted by his guard. He'd been nothing but cordial, and provided a fine facsimile of freedom for most of the time that Hathar had been wandering the palace, but it was very clear that Hathar was being held captive.

He looked down at the book in his hands. *The Caged Heart.*

WHEN HATHAR RETURNED to the dayroom, Elin was there, curled up into a corner of a richly upholstered sofa and gazing out at the sky.

From the sound of it, several of the other men were playing a spirited game of cards in the dining room. The rest must be napping, or out in the garden, because the room was otherwise unoccupied.

Hathar walked quietly over to where Elin sat and reached out to run a hand tenderly up his arm and onto his shoulder.

Elin jolted out of his contemplations and looked up, eyes widening as he registered Hathar's face.

"You're here," he said softly, his mouth curving into a tentative smile.

Hathar laughed a little. "I don't know if you've noticed, but it doesn't seem like any of us are allowed to be anywhere else."

Elin thought about that for a moment. "No. No, of course not. It's just...you said yesterday that you hoped you wouldn't be missing the sea too long, and when I couldn't find you after breakfast, I thought maybe you'd left."

Hathar flopped down next to him with a sigh. "How would I leave? You were wrong when you said this place wasn't a jail. It's a pleasant jail, very fine, but no one's about to let me just wander out the front door because I'm tired of the party."

He leaned over to look Elin in the eye. "Does this mean you're talking to me again, then?"

Elin blushed at that. "I wasn't not talking to you."

"No?" He let the question hang between them, waiting for an answer.

"I mean, I guess I wasn't *talking* to you, either. I just..." Elin looked out the window again. "I didn't want you to think that I thought you owed me anything after last night. I know these things happen. I won't chase you around expecting your attention all the time."

His words put a weight on Hathar's heart. "I'm pretty sure I have some extra attention I can spare. Would you come for a walk with me?" He stood, holding out a hand.

Elin reached up to take it, a warm glow kindling in his amber eyes.

They headed out over the veranda and down the stairs to the garden, veering away from the perpetual wrestling match on the lawn near the wall, instead following a path through ornamental plantings and pornographic statuary.

"So where were you when you weren't escaping?" Elin asked once they seemed to be out of earshot of the other men.

"I just took myself on a little tour of the palace."

Elin's brows drew together, and he scrunched up his nose at that. "Really? Why? No one bothers to go out there unless it's a feast day or something. It's just a bunch of big empty rooms."

"Yes, well, I see I should have talked to you first."

Hathar considered what he wanted to say next. A part of him, the same part that quaked now each time they touched, wanted to confide in Elin, to throw his predicament at his feet and ask for help, beg him to join in whatever would be next. The rest of him— made cynical by the petty betrayals and more serious backstabbings of a life of merchant adventuring—screamed to keep his mouth shut and his head down. Tender feelings were all very well, but not worth risking his life and his crew over.

He needed a compromise, a small confession with limited repercussions that he could use to evaluate Elin's trustworthiness.

"I was looking for some coin," he said, resolved.

"Coeen?" Elin asked, drawing out the word uncertainly.

"You know, gold, silver, maybe even a snuffbox or a statuette. Something I could use to bribe a low-level menial to get me out of here. Maybe someone in the kitchens."

Elin stared at him for a long moment, clearly baffled.

"We don't have anything like that here," he finally worked out. "The Dragon doesn't allow it."

"She doesn't...? But that's what dragons are all about! Does she take it all to hoard in a cave or something? A secret vault? What do the common people use for money?"

"Oh no, no, no vaults. She got rid of it all, I think, when she first arrived, centuries ago. She's a very devout follower of Helcamet, who delights in the erotic. She gave up the pleasures of treasure for the pleasures of the flesh as a gesture of her devotion. Doesn't allow the temptation anywhere in the kingdom.

"We don't have any need for money here in the haram since everything is provided, but my understanding is that the people in town use paper notes for trade."

"Paper? Like..." Hathar made a vague gesture with thumb and forefinger. "Just paper?"

"Well, made for the purpose, with an image of The Dragon and intricate patterns that would be hard to reproduce. But yes, just paper." Elin seemed to lose himself in thought for a moment and then continued. "I suppose as long as they all agree that it's worth something, it is."

This was a blow. Far beyond bribes, Hathar was here for treasure. His men, his whole crew was here, waiting just out of sight offshore for treasure. If there was none... Well, there was nothing for it. He still had to get out of here and let them know. They wouldn't be any better off leaving without riches *or* captain.

Elin seemed to pick up on the dark turn in Hathar's mood and stopped walking, turning to place a hand on his arm. "Are you all right?"

"I just..." Hathar trailed off and seemed to be cataloging something in his head. "I'm an idiot. Wooden forks, glass razors, doors with guards instead of keys and locks... I should have put it all together. But who expects a dragon to be some kind of twisted ascetic?"

"I'm maybe not the best person to ask," Elin replied seriously. "I've only ever known the one."

This, in the face of such a ridiculous, unforeseen upset, struck Hathar as blackly hilarious. He began to chuckle, to guffaw, and then to simply heave silently as laughter overwhelmed him. Gasping for breath, he clutched the bewildered Elin to himself for support, rested his head on Elin's shoulder, and laughed until tears came, soaking the fabric of his shirt. He laughed for minutes until he was finally able to choke out, "Indeed. I suppose that's so."

Chapter Five

THAT NIGHT, ELIN woke to a tickling sensation on his foot where it protruded from the blankets.

He started, and looked down to find Hathar standing at the bottom of the bed, running a finger back and forth over his arch and radiating mischief. When they made eye contact, he beckoned and nodded his head in the direction of the door.

Stealthily as he could, Elin slithered out of his place in the shared bed and followed Hathar out to the dayroom.

The room was empty, everyone else asleep. Guards, as always, were posted outside the doors, but they didn't bother to observe their charges directly in the night. Moonlight filtered in, just barely illuminating the furnishings and allowing the two men to see one another.

As the door closed behind them, Hathar reached out to take Elin's hand and pulled him swiftly into a warm embrace, aligning their naked bodies from knee to chest and giving just the slightest suggestive thrust of his hips.

"I was hoping you'd let me repay you for your kind attentions last night," Hathar whispered, causing the hairs on the back of Elin's neck to rise. His skin where they touched was impossibly hot in the cool night air of the room.

Hathar ran a large, calloused hand down from Elin's shoulder to take a hearty grasp of his buttock, squeezing appreciatively and placing a series of moist kisses over the sensitive pulse points of his throat and along his jaw, finally arriving at his mouth. Elin opened to meet him without the slightest hesitation this time, reveling in the contact of their tongues and encouraging Hathar to explore him thoroughly.

A pleasurable pressure built where their growing erections nudged together as they kissed and petted. Hathar brought a hand between them to gently grasp Elin's cock, but as he did so, Elin started slightly and broke off the kiss. Stopping immediately, Hathar put both hands on Elin's shoulders and held him a little ways back, the better to look at him.

Hathar frowned, and his brows drew low over his eyes as he asked softly, "What is it?"

Elin looked down and away, unable to meet Hathar's gaze.

When he didn't respond, Hathar coaxed, "It's all right. I don't think there's a thing you could say that would shock or offend a scallywag of my stripe. You don't have to talk to me, but... If you'd tell me what to do differently, I'd really, *really* like a chance to make you feel even half as good as you made me feel last night, if...you know...that's something you even want."

"I do," Elin whispered, still looking down.

Hathar smiled hopefully at that. "So... tell me how to please you."

Finally, Elin looked up. He hoped Hathar might not notice the tears he could feel pricking at his eyes.

"You do please me. You please me so much, I—" His voice failed, and he took a breath.

"I'm just afraid. I've never felt any of this before, and I'm so used to saying no that it feels terrifying to say yes." He came closer to Hathar again, seeking comfort against his firm chest.

Hathar drew them both down to sit on the velvet divan. He wore a thoughtful expression that suggested he was putting the pieces together. "Have you not lain with a man before?" he asked gently.

Elin started to shudder with silent laughter. His guess was so close to the mark, and yet so desperately far afield. At last, shaking his head, he said, "I've never lain with anyone—done anything with anyone, other than the little bit I've done with you."

"But— In a haram? I thought you had to serve The Dragon? You said you weren't one of her favorites, but how could she let a treasure like you go completely untouched?"

Elin sighed and tilted his head back to stare at the ceiling, his body going limp with resignation. "There's a reason I was sent to help you in the baths instead of someone like Larin or Marik. I'm given tasks like that because...well, The Dragon doesn't have any use for me. I don't get called up to her service like the others."

"Doesn't have any use for you?! Does she have a brain in her head? You're worth a dozen Mariks!" Hathar erupted.

"Shh! I appreciate your outrage on my behalf, but let's not wake anyone." Elin was both touched and shocked by Hathar's outburst. After so long at the bottom of the heap, it was foreign to think that anyone could prefer him. Though he hoped Hathar had chosen him because he felt the same pull as Elin, a large part of him believed he'd only been graced with the newcomer's attention because Hathar had been so soundly rejected by the rest of the cohort.

"Anyway," Elin said, shifting to lie with his head in Hathar's lap, his legs curling over the arm of the divan, "she has her reasons..."

And so, Elin told Hathar the story of his single, ill-fated trip to the chambers of The Dragon, tentatively at first, but gaining confidence in the face of Hathar's unwavering interest.

"You puked on her," he said reverently as the story concluded. "Serves her right, too. Trying to treat you like some kind of sex slave when you were scared shitless."

Elin cringed at that. "But it isn't just her. She was kind really, within the bounds of what was expected between us. She tried to be gentle. I just...I've felt that way about everyone, every sexual thing, the games the other men would get up to...until you.

"And so, as good as it feels and as much as I suddenly want this, I'm used to panicking, and it's a really hard impulse to kill. Thinking that I might make a mistake and horrify you and drive you away, or you might do the wrong thing, when I don't even know what the wrong thing is— I just want to shrivel up and blow away."

"Hey," Hathar said soothingly, petting Elin's hair. "Don't go blowing away on me just yet. Can we try again?"

Elin nodded. "I'd like to."

"Okay. I want you to know that you're safe with me. If you say stop, I'll stop, and I won't be pissy about it. If you panic, I'll help calm you down, and I won't let my feelings get all bent out of shape. If you puke on me...well...I guess I'll let you give me another bath."

Elin laughed at that, and it was a genuine laugh this time, born of relief at sharing a secret that had caused him so much shame and finding only acceptance and good humor. He reached up and brought Hathar's face down for a slightly awkward, hunching kiss, through which he nonetheless tried to express all his relief and joy and gratitude.

"So, how are we going to do this?" Hathar asked, looking to Elin for guidance.

"Let's move over there," he suggested, gesturing to a large round chair in a corner, sized to easily fit two or more, and more comfortable than the rigid divan.

Elin settled there on his back, his head and shoulders propped up on a cushion, only his feet and ankles extending beyond the generous seat. Hathar was close behind, but hesitated a little, standing as if awaiting further instruction.

"Come down here," Elin suggested. "I'm not sure what to ask for, but just...take it slow? I think it'll be okay now."

Hathar bent and slid himself up onto the seat, straddling Elin, just grazing their bodies together on his way past. He started again with soft and tender kisses until Elin's response began to hint of desperation. With a final nip at Elin's lips, Hathar moved on to his chest.

He started with a lick, a nibble, a gentle suck, and was rewarded with a moan of pleasure from Elin, who arched back against the cushion and writhed deliciously.

"That okay?" Hathar asked, his lips still hovering just above Elin's nipple.

"So okay," Elin replied, his voice barely a whisper, eyes half closed.

Hathar licked his thumb and forefinger and used them to mimic the actions of his mouth and tongue on the other side of Elin's chest, doubling the sensation for a moment.

He trailed his free hand down Elin's ribs and followed it with his mouth, placing a series of hot, sucking kisses down his flank. He continued further down, a little slower and gentler now, making his way to the fold where Elin's thigh met his body, tracing that line with the tip of his slick tongue.

Elin jolted at that first contact of a mouth so near his cock, but immediately relaxed with a small sigh that trailed off into a murmur of pleasure.

"Still okay?" Hathar was nuzzling his stubbled cheek against Elin's inner thigh as he asked.

"Mmmhmm," was the lazy but emphatic reply. Elin reached down to give Hathar's hair a clumsy stroke and lifted his pelvis slightly in encouragement.

He was hard now, and Hathar gazed admiringly at the profile of Elin's cock as it was silhouetted against the moonlit window, the partially exposed head shining with moisture. Hathar buried his nose in the golden curls at its root, and then lifted himself a little to tenderly take just the first few inches into his mouth.

The sensation was unlike anything Elin had ever experienced. It was the intimate, slippery wrangling of a kiss, but expressed on the most sensitive part of his anatomy. He gasped as Hathar lapped in unhurried circles, and had to choke back a shout when that sensation was intensified by a single finger running down the cleft between his buttocks to tease the border of his rear entrance and continue along between his legs.

Hathar licked and sucked his way down, little by little, until he held Elin's full length in his mouth. He looked up then, and Elin answered the question in his glance with what he hoped was an expression of lust. Hathar worked his lips up and down in a leisurely rhythm, echoed by his fingers behind. Elin's mouth dropped open and his eyes closed as he was caught up in his increasing pleasure.

He gave himself over fully to sensation, fear tamed and driven wild simultaneously by Hathar's touch. A sudden change of pace suggested that Hathar was about to lose control himself. He reached down to take his own cock in his free hand and began to pump urgently, increasing the speed of his mouth on Elin to keep up.

In moments, they were both undone: Elin gasping as he spent, Hathar just behind, seemingly pushed over the brink by the warm flood of semen in his mouth, his own load showering over Elin's lower half and lightly spattering the upholstery between his legs.

Strength sapped, Hathar collapsed, his head resting on Elin's thigh. Both men were silent but for their heavy breathing and the pounding of their hearts.

As their pulses slowed, Hathar climbed wearily up to where Elin lay, drawing a throw over them both and wrapping their bodies snugly together.

"Better than okay," Elin whispered as he melted into Hathar's embrace and sleep claimed him.

THE FIRST FINGERS of golden sunlight were creeping over the mountains when Elin next opened his eyes. It took him a moment to get his bearings, but a flush of elation washed over him as he remembered why he was waking up in the dayroom, with Hathar's bulk still wrapped protectively around him, rather than his own bed.

That elation drained swiftly to a cold dread in the pit of his stomach as he registered several faces looming over him. They had been discovered.

Elin tried to pretend he hadn't noticed, to roll over and feign sleep in hopes the others would lose interest and wander off. No such luck. A moment later, someone kicked the chair, jarring it violently and causing Hathar to sit up with a start, dislodging Elin and forcing him to sit up as well.

"You fellas need something?" Hathar asked, looking up at them blearily.

Ignoring him to focus instead on Elin, the short, bulky man named Kiran spat, "Can't get it up for The Dragon, but you'll bend over for some white-eyed foreigner as soon as he looks at you, eh?"

"I—" Elin began.

But Rian interjected, "Fucking disgusting. He's not even proper *dahabi*. You may be an embarrassment to the haram, but at least try to have a little pride in your birth."

Some of the others jeered inarticulately, and Neril came around and flicked Hathar's ear in a childish gesture, which earned him a shove. As voices rose in protest, Elin found his words.

"You're ridiculous. Pride in my birth? Pride at what? Having the right hair color to be kidnapped for life in captivity? I'll take my pride in choosing what I want for myself and having the nerve to go after it, thanks." His hand tightened where it rested on Hathar's thigh as he continued.

"You're just a bunch of petty, narcissistic children! Take your '*dahabi*' and shove it. There's no glory in a title that labels me in any way the same as the rest of you."

A few of the men had already begun to recede at this uncharacteristic outburst. This was not the dreamy, vague Elin they had expected to easily cow.

"Go on," he said. "I'm sure you have some really important dick-measuring to attend to."

"Disgrace!" Kiran hissed, dealing the chair one last kick as the congregation slid away toward breakfast.

"So...good morning, then," Hathar said with a sigh once they were more or less alone.

"Sorry. They're idiots, but you already knew that. They won't really do anything. The Dragon doesn't tolerate anyone harming her *dahabi,* including other *dahabi.* None of them would want to jeopardize their place in her favor over us. At least...I think."

"That'd be wise of them," Hathar replied. "Because I don't give a shit about The Dragon's favor, and I'd be happy to get kicked out of here if I could take a few of those punks with me."

Elin looked at him seriously. "Don't do that. They're not worth it, really, and I'd much rather have you here with me. It's not like she would just set you free, anyway. We belong to her. No one mentions the details, but I get the impression that some kind of confinement is involved when men are removed from their cohorts. It's not a good thing."

"Okay, all right..." Hathar's expression softened as he saw the real concern on Elin's face. He reached out and placed a hand on his shoulder.

"That was pretty impressive, what you said there. Did you see how the fight just kinda drained out of them?" He smirked and continued. "I want to say, 'I didn't think you had it in ya,' but that's not right. I suspected you had it in you, but I wasn't sure you wanted to let everybody know."

Elin blushed at that and looked a little uncomfortable. "I didn't do anything," he said with a shrug.

"Hey! You kept me from beating that kid who was messing with my ear to a bloody pulp. That's something. The Dragon should give you a medal for preventing the spill of so much precious *dahabi* blood." Hathar grinned and gave Elin a squeeze. "Come on. We've still got some cleaning up to do from last night. How about *I* bathe *you* this time?"

Hathar stood and dragged Elin up behind him, a resigned smile starting to take shape on the smaller man's face.

Chapter Six

THINGS WERE DIFFERENT after that morning.

Between Hathar and Elin, it was as if a wall had come down. In turn, however, a new wall between them and the rest of the cohort had been erected.

Elin was used to being an afterthought among his peers, but being casually overlooked was a very different sensation than feeling everyone's attention focused pointedly *away* from him. He was no longer welcome in the bed with Rian and Nikil but was happy enough to leave them to it and join Hathar on the floor of the alcove.

His prediction that the other men would be unlikely to resort to violence, that the stakes were too high, seemed to have proven correct. This was a cold war, a shunning. Elin had a vague notion he should be more hurt than he was. These men were, after all, the closest thing to family he had. He'd lived with them since before conscious memory.

And yet... After a week's acquaintance, he felt more kinship, acceptance, and trust with Hathar than he'd known in his life to date.

"TELL ME MORE about the sea," Elin asked. He and Hathar were lounging near the fountain in the wooded part of the garden, in what he'd come to think of as "their" place: the one spot they were reasonably assured of some peace and privacy from the whispered taunts and disapproving sidelong glances that otherwise followed them.

Hathar chuckled indulgently. They had covered the animals—the great grey whales singing songs beneath the waves that caused the very timbers of the ship to hum, and the spritely dolphins that would materialize out of nowhere to leap and spin in the wake. They'd spoken of the changeability of the weather—red skies and seething storms that could reduce masts to splinters, so different from the repetitive balmy pleasantness of Minal'taneen, and they'd covered the exotic ports and peoples, with their fascinating customs and foods and modes of dress.

"What more do you want to know?"

Elin twined his fingers absently in the silky strands of Hathar's hair as he thought, relishing the weight of his lover's head in his lap. "Tell me about your boat," he said, finally.

"My boat..." Hathar repeated. "Well, first of all, she's a ship. A ship can carry a boat, but a boat can't carry a ship, you know." Elin did not know but he nodded, encouraging Hathar to go on.

"She's a three-masted fluyt. My father's, originally. He was an excellent trader. Very methodical. He had his route, and he stuck to it, year in and year out. Kept perfect books. He could tell you how much he made on a bale of raw cotton any time in the last twenty year, if you just gave him a moment to consult his ledgers.

"He named her *The Prudent Mistress*. I've often wondered what my mother thought of that, but she died of fever when I was only a few years old, so I never got the chance to ask."

Elin's brow furrowed. He didn't have much of a memory of his own mother, of course, having been delivered to The Dragon at not much more than two years old, but he still felt a pang at the thought of tiny Hathar going through such a loss.

"I sailed with Dad after that. Not a bad way to grow up really, with the whole world as your classroom. Lacking a little for playmates, maybe, but he kept me busy, and I did have a monkey for a while."

"A monkey?"

"Yeah. Cute little thing. Used to steal treasures and bring them back to me. Of course...a monkey's idea of treasure... Sometimes it was a nice stone or a piece of broken glass, sometimes coins or brooches. Once he proudly presented me with three brass buttons from the coat of a wealthy merchant who'd come to meet with Dad. That took some explaining." He laughed at the memory and trailed off, staring up past Elin into the cloudless sky.

"So then," Elin prompted, "you took over from your dad at some point?"

"Right." A shadow fell over Hathar's expression as he continued.

"About six years ago. I tried to do things like he did—stick to the route, keep the records...but I was never like him in that way. So, merchant adventuring, right? We still trade—pick up whatever's cheap in one place and bring it along to the next, but I keep an ear out for other opportunities as well. Maybe a ship went missing with all its cargo. If it's wrecked and we can find it, that could bring us as much gold as we'd make in a year doing things Dad's way. Of course, it's hit and miss. You can spend months chasing a rumor with nothing to show for it. It probably sounds mad to say that that's part of the fun, but there it is. It's a gamble!"

The conversation, for Elin, was taking an abrupt turn from the abstract to the concrete. Merchant adventuring, chasing rumors... "Is that how you came here then? Was Minal'taneen one of your 'opportunities'?"

Hathar looked...what was that look? A little ashamed, maybe? He didn't seem to want to say whatever was coming next.

"Well...yes. I didn't know I would find you here, of course."

"What *were* you looking for? I don't think we get much in the way of wrecked ships around here. The weather's always so calm. For that matter, as far as I know, what little trade there is comes through the mountains."

Hathar gave him a meaningful look. "Did you ever wonder why that is? You're in a beautiful town on an idyllic harbor, and no one makes use of it but a few local fishermen? No traders? Not even an occasional lost craft?"

It was not a subject that Elin had given any real consideration to. He had no need to think about the economy or trade, no experience of any other town or port for comparison. "I can't say I've really thought about it, but I suppose The Dragon kept them away. Traders would bring metal, right? She wouldn't have that."

"Correct!" Hathar sat up. "I didn't know the part about the metal. I thought the whole point was to hide great heaping mounds of gold and treasure, but your dragon has had the whole port masked by magic. When you look at it from out at sea, all you see is a completely uninteresting rocky shore. Not just uninteresting in the way of rocky shores, but as if your attention almost...slips off it."

Elin gave him a long, appraising look. "Are you making things up to amuse yourself now? I know I may seem naive, but The Dragon does educate us. The only magic I'm aware of is the kind that happens in stories."

"Says the man who lives in the palace of a flying serpent who chooses to spend most of her time in the form of a human woman." Hathar smirked at him.

"But that's different. Isn't it? I mean..." Elin focused inward. "Well, when you say it that way, it does sound a little farfetched. I guess I'm just used to The Dragon's particular flavor of magic. It seems much more reasonable than being asked to believe that an entire city is protected by a magical illusion. And besides!" He focused on Hathar. "If that's true, how are you here? Why aren't you out in the middle of the ocean ignoring the uninteresting rocky beach?"

"Ah!" Hathar grinned devilishly, and his eyes sparkled. "Now that is a story!

"So, onboard *The Prudent Mistress*, we make our money as we can, and will from time to time take on a passenger who happens to be headed to wherever we're already going. We were about to set sail from Ostund, completely laden with reeking barrels of fermented fish oil headed south, when a lad came running down the docks begging for a ride. I tried to put him off. Told him the smell would have him retching over the side before we left port, but he insisted that he had fine sea legs and needed to be in Arelles in a week. He said he'd pay what I asked, and to sweeten the deal, he'd sing for us every night at sea. He was a minstrel, you see, lute on his back. I relented and let him board, and it wasn't just because he was a beautiful thing, which he was, though not half such a beautiful thing as you."

Elin rolled his eyes but inwardly preened a little.

"My intuition was nagging me to have this lad aboard. I couldn't say what I thought he might bring to us, but I had a feeling that he might somehow be important.

"So the first night was uneventful. He sang, as promised. Had a fine enough voice. It was a nice diversion for the men to have some entertainment in the evening.

"The next night was the same, but as things were winding down for the night he offered one last song. It wasn't one I'd ever heard before, and I didn't pay it much attention at first. It was a ballad, a little slow and mournful. The right sort of thing to send everyone off to bed.

"I'd had a bit to drink, and might have even been dozing a little where I sat, but I snapped out of it when I caught the chorus of his song— *Between the lion and the serpent lies the lusty dragon queen, lies by night atop her treasure hidden in Minal'taneen.*

"I looked around the room, but everyone else was still listening with the same lazy indifference I'd felt a moment before. Of course, they didn't know what I did. You get a lot of turnover on a ship like mine, and none of the crew was the same as served my father back when I was twelve—when we were caught in a storm on an unfamiliar route. He'd taken on a special job, which was out of character, and the sea whipped up in a way no one was expecting when we were only a few nights in. We were able to ride it out, but by the time things calmed, we were far off course in unknown waters."

Elin shuddered, shaken by the notion of being lost and adrift. The walls he'd been raised within didn't leave room to become even mildly disoriented.

"As we sailed, trying to get our bearings, we came within sight of land. The first thing I remember seeing, as the coast came into view, were two huge rocky outcroppings—one in the shape of a lion, lying down, head up and paws outstretched, the other seeming to be a serpent slithering down to the beach from the mountains above. It made an impression, both because the shapes were so striking and unusual, seeming to be natural formations but still so clear and lifelike, and because the sight of any land, after the unsettling sensation of being lost at sea, was such a relief to my young mind. My father was a very careful seaman, so I'd had little experience of that kind of uncertainty under his care.

"So when I heard that chorus, I knew he was singing of the place I'd chanced upon so many years before. Not only that, but he was singing of treasure there. I listened intently to the rest of the song and tried to commit as much of it as I could to memory.

"I had the minstrel end each night with *The Dragon Queen* after that. I said that it sent me off to pleasant dreams, which was true enough as I was dreaming of riches for us all, but didn't let on that it was anything more to me than a song.

"There wasn't much to it. Most of the verses were just sweetly sung smut, in the style of some of the bawdier ballads. Other than the chorus, it was the last verse that struck me as meaningful. *If you wish to go and find her, to be taken to her bed, you must try to come in sideways, can't be forging straight ahead. For those that go a-looking find a pile of rocks instead, think not of what you see but see that place where you'd be led.*

"The day before we were to part ways, I took the minstrel aside and asked what he knew of the song. By then it was clear to him that I had some special fondness for it, and I told him I'd never heard it before, which I found remarkable when so many minstrels seemed to travel here and there, all singing the same handful of tunes.

"He said he'd learned it off an elderly harper whose voice was too rough to sing anymore. They'd crossed paths years back, out near the edge of the continent, and it seemed that the harper was from even further afield originally. From the south, the minstrel thought, by the sound of his accent.

"I pressed him for all he knew, but there seemed to be nothing more to it. Still, this little information fueled my excitement, because it was far to the south that we'd been lost, so long ago, which strengthened my conviction that I'd been within a league or so of this hidden treasure trove.

"Once we parted ways, I went to my father's beautiful, meticulous logs and found the record of that day. I charted the original path and from that found our approximate location on the day the storm hit. It was then a matter of looking around for land within a reasonable distance of that spot, that we might have reached with two days aimless bobbing at sea. I was able to narrow my search down to a stretch off the far southeast coast of the Southern Sea.

"I had to proceed carefully. I didn't want my men to become overexcited on a hunch, or worse yet, for one of them to run off and try to sell my hunch to someone else. I took my time, going ashore whenever we came to a place big enough to have a library. I learned what I could about dragons, but I couldn't find anything specifically about the mythical city of Minal'taneen."

It was strange for Elin to think that his home was someone else's myth. As far as he was concerned, it was the world beyond that might still prove to be mythical.

"I quietly pressed us farther south, trading in the islands of the western Southern Sea. Working slowly east along the coast, it didn't seem too out of order to suggest that we continue on a little farther 'to see what we would see.'

"By the charts, I was taking us to a mostly deserted part of the coast, but wrecks wash up everywhere, and sometimes settlements crop up where you'd least expect them, so the men made no complaint.

"We sailed on, in sight of land, and just as I was starting to feel like I'd been led on a wild-goose chase by my own idiot intuition, I saw the stone serpent come into view, exactly as I remembered it.

The lion followed right behind, with a stretch of rocky beach between. This was it! What I'd been searching for! And yet...I couldn't quite bring myself to tell the men. It was like my brain didn't trust my eyes, or maybe the other way around. I knew what I was seeing, but at the same time, I wasn't sure that what I was seeing was what I was looking for.

"I gave the order to drop anchor and set the crew to work on some routine maintenance to give myself some time to think. If they thought it odd that I stopped in the middle of nowhere to scrape barnacles, they didn't dare say it to my face.

"I took to my cabin for a while to consider my options, and finally emerged, calling on a couple of my best men to launch a dinghy and accompany me on a jaunt to the shore. That did earn me a few curious looks, but I simply said I had a hunch and left it at that.

"On board the dinghy, I set Jaren on the oars and told him to head for the beach between the two stone outcroppings. He started out strong, but shortly started to flag and asked me if I was sure of where we were going. I started to bark at him that of course I was sure, but as I looked at the beach, I couldn't shake the feeling that I wasn't sure at all. Still, I was captain. I told him to carry on as I'd said.

"He really did try, but it seemed like he couldn't hold a steady course. He'd hesitate—veer this way and that. I could see that he was confused and his confidence was shaken. I told the other man, Rath, to take over for a while, but he was strangely reluctant, telling me that this all seemed like a lot of trouble for nothing, that he could tell from here there was nothing on shore for us but a bunch of useless rocks. Despite myself, I found that I agreed. I couldn't even choke out the order to proceed. I relented, and told him to take us back to the ship. As we turned around, the tension that had been building on our little craft evaporated almost immediately.

"Back on board, my head was clearer. I'd been a fool, of course. The song was clear as day. It told me not to go forging straight ahead. My experience of magic to that point was about like yours—none—so I'd thought the thing about coming in sideways was advice on wooing, not navigation. I resolved to try again, myself, by night. I thought it would be easier to keep my own mind on track, without anyone else there to reinforce the doubts I was now sure would greet me as I neared my goal.

"It was a full moon that night, and the dinghy was still in the water. I set out, but this time, set my sights to one side, to the unshielded beach south of the stone serpent. As long as I kept my focus to the south, everything was fine, but when I glanced toward my true goal, I could feel the uncertainty and confusion creeping back in.

"I continued in that way until I was within a hundred yards of shore and then stopped to consider my next move. I turned the boat to face the beach between the stones. From this angle, it still wasn't easy to focus on, but I could kind of gaze out past it so that the rocks were just caught in the edge of my vision, and that felt better.

"I tried to remember the rest of the song as I inched closer to the beach on a long, shallow angle. *Think not of what you see but see that place where you'd be led.* Of course, I didn't really know what the place I was looking for would look like, but I tried to hold the idea of a coastal city in my mind. There would be docks and boats, small buildings running up from the water, the palace probably up the hill and backing it all up. As I got closer, that peripheral image of the beach seemed to flicker, letting through split-second impressions of something else. I tried to focus on what I could make out, pushing aside the doubt that intensified even as evidence I was on the right track presented itself. I willed myself on, stroke by stroke, feeling mad with the simultaneous certainty that I was on the completely wrong track and that I was about to reach my goal.

"Finally, it was as if something snapped. With a stroke of my oars, I felt myself pop through an invisible barrier, and suddenly, all doubt was gone. I was there, in my dinghy, in a quiet moonlit port. The only vessels at the dock were small fishing craft."

The awe in Hathar's face was clear to see as he relived the moment. Elin no longer had any doubt that he'd experienced real magic.

"The town was much as I'd imagined. Quite unremarkable, other than the magical concealment.

Just a seaside city like a hundred others I'd visited. Even The Dragon's palace, my ultimate goal, followed a common plan.

"Now that I'd done it once and knew what I was looking for, I was certain I could make it through again. I turned back in the direction of my ship and was surprised to see nothing there. Of course, the people of Minal'taneen had to be equally convinced there was nothing interesting beyond the bounds of their little harbor to keep them from venturing out and getting stuck beyond the barrier. I knew my ship was there though, and that confidence helped me to press on until I felt the same popping sensation and it flashed into view.

"The next day, I took my officers into my confidence. I told them the song was true, and that the rocky beach was only an illusion to conceal the town where the mythical dragon kept her hoard. I ordered them to anchor the ship in the next cove over, where the shield didn't reach, while I went ashore to learn the location of the treasure and concoct a plan for us to return to make off with it. I told them to give me a fortnight, which seemed like plenty of time to case the palace, and if I hadn't returned in that time, that my second could take up the command and do as he saw fit.

"And so…" Hathar gestured to take in the present scene.

Elin had been absorbing Hathar's story with a rapt expression. "So this has all been part of your plan? You got yourself taken into the haram to case the palace?"

"Oh! No. That…was a surprise. I was wandering around outside, trying to look like any other passerby, when the city guard took me down."

"Because you're so fair."

"Apparently."

Elin thought for a minute.

"So, you've been here a little over a week. If you're not out in another week, what will your second do?"

Hathar heaved a heavy sigh. "He's a good man. He'll probably try to launch a rescue, but I can't expect them to make it through the barrier. I assume they'll give it their best shot, and then have to set off and leave me here."

Elin's heart lurched at that. There was a dark, selfish little part of him that would dearly love for Hathar to be trapped here in the haram with him. He could think of worse things than a lifetime of the two of them taking refuge in one another in uncomplicated, if somewhat restrictive, luxury. But Hathar could never really be satisfied with that. Elin had seen how the palace walls chafed him after only a few days. What damage would months or years do?

He reached out and took Hathar's hands in his own.

"So we have to get you out," he said simply.

Hathar smiled wistfully at that and drew him close. "That's about the size of it. There are a few things I'd like to do before I go though."

He kissed Elin then, and in that kiss was tenderness, and longing, and a bittersweet acknowledgment that their remaining time might be short. Elin clutched at Hathar's shirt, at his shoulders, crossed his arms tight around his neck, deepening the kiss. He knew, in that moment, that whenever Hathar went, he wanted to go too.

Chapter Seven

THE NEXT DAY at breakfast, Hathar seemed particularly interested in the flow of dishes to and from the kitchen. Elin didn't exactly notice, at first, used as he was to keeping himself company at meals. But when he saw that Hathar, usually ravenous, still had an almost entirely untouched plate in front of him and was focused more on the servants than his now-congealed eggs, he became curious.

He nudged Hathar under the table where their thighs met and asked quietly, "What's so interesting?"

His eyes still on a stack of plates being whisked away through the discreet service door in the dining room wall, Hathar muttered, "How many kitchens do you suppose the palace has?"

Elin's brow furrowed as he considered that. "One? I don't know why you'd need any more. The palace is large, but it would make the most sense to have all the cooking consolidated in one place."

"Right," Hathar agreed.

"Nice day for a walk," he added, in a seeming non-sequitur. "Will you join me in the garden after we eat?"

Elin narrowed his eyes and raised an eyebrow but took an unhurried sip of his dark, syrupy coffee. "I'd be delighted."

As they strolled near the wall, Hathar began, "So, if those service corridors run to the kitchen, and the kitchen has to be able to serve the whole palace, then, in theory, you could get from our wing to anywhere else in the building that way."

Elin considered that for a couple of steps. "Sure, but haven't you already seen the palace? There's nothing there, remember?"

"Ah!" Hathar threw an arm casually around Elin's shoulder to bring him close as they walked. "But that was the *public* part of the palace. What do you think The Dragon might be hiding in her private chambers?"

Elin stopped then and turned, wide-eyed, to stare at Hathar.

"You're not serious."

Hathar took Elin's hand and dragged him gently toward the wooded portion of the garden. "Let's not draw too much attention to ourselves," he said, pinning Elin against the smooth, knobby bark of a tree trunk, one hand on either side of his head. Hathar leaned in for a kiss, some of Elin's shocked stiffness unwinding at the tender contact. He then leaned in further still to whisper into his ear, "The song said The Dragon 'sleeps by night atop her treasure.' I assumed that was sort of figurative, but there's no treasure anywhere else, so maybe not. There could be something where she sleeps—literally under the bed. I've got to at least take a look." He ran his fingers through Elin's curls, and kissed him again lightly. Anyone observing would think they were exchanging sweet nothings.

"But..." Elin couldn't immediately put into words what he feared, he knew only that the direction of Hathar's thoughts was filling him with a cold dread. "What about the guards?" He grasped at the first obstacle that came to hand.

"I've never seen the guards paying any attention to the service doors. Have you? As long as it's between meal times, and everyone else is otherwise occupied, I think I can just slip through."

Elin had to admit that the guards mainly focused on the outer doors, or lurked unobtrusively wherever the men were congregated. If Hathar made his move when the dayroom was empty, he could probably get away with it. Once on the other side though...

"What about the servants? Even if you choose a time when no one should be headed to our wing, any number of people could be bustling around back there. For all we know, you might have to walk directly through the kitchens to get to The Dragon's chambers."

Hathar smirked. "I'll be careful, but if I run into anyone, I'll just...tell them I got lost, or that I'm looking for a snack or something. I'm new! And I'm *dahabi*, I guess. They're not going to do anything to me other than turn me around and show me back to our quarters. Probably even make me a sandwich. You shoulda seen that guard that was stalking me when I went on my little recon mission. Looked like he might piss himself when he thought he was actually going to have to get stern with me."

Elin tipped his head forward to rest it wearily on Hathar's shoulder.

"And The Dragon?" he muttered.

He felt Hathar's weight shift.

"Well, I'll just have to go when I know she won't be there." He was missing a little of his previous confidence.

Elin shook his head against the fabric of Hathar's shirt. "But you're new. You don't know when that is. You won't even know for sure if you've found the right room or not because you've never been there." After a long moment, he heaved a sigh, his head still down. "I should go."

Hathar's expression said that it was now his turn to feel dread. Elin leaned back against the tree and went on.

"I know where I'm going, and if I'm caught, I can invent some sort of suitably genteel errand to be on. The guards are always using me for that sort of thing."

"But you don't know what you're looking for," Hathar objected.

"Just peek under the bed, right? How hard can that be?"

"But it's not just going to be heaped there for the taking. There will be a hidden hatch, a magical lock, some kind of secret compartment. You need experience to know that kind of thing when you see it. How many palaces have you pillaged?"

Elin cocked his head. "How many palaces have *you* pillaged?" It seemed there might be more to "merchant adventuring" than just hunting down wrecks.

"Enough. But that's a story for another time." Hathar ran his hands affectionately down Elin's flanks.

Elin should have been shocked, but he couldn't quite muster it with Hathar's hands so warm and firm on his body. "All right," he said, "so we both go. If we're caught on the way, I can say I was asked to escort you to discuss the menu with the cook—to see about adding some dishes from your homeland."

Hathar smiled and moved his hands to Elin's buttocks, pulling their hips together.

"All right my most knowledgeable Elin, scholar of all matters pertaining to the inner workings of the palace of Minal'taneen, pray tell when we might be assured that The Dragon's chambers will be left vacant."

"Well," Elin began, pausing to run his lips over the delicious rasp of Hathar's stubbled jaw, "it just so happens that today is Wednesday, and on Wednesday, The Dragon hosts a luncheon for the town dignitaries. The *dahabi* cohorts take turns attending. This week is the thirty-fourth's turn, so we're off the hook. And what's more, on luncheon days, everyone else gets to graze on cold plates for lunch so that the staff can focus on the guests, so as long as we wait until our wing has been served, there shouldn't be much traffic in the service corridors. We just have to get back before they come to clean up."

"Auspicious! It's like it was meant to be." Hathar gave him a fervent kiss, vibrating now with anticipation. "So when do we set out?"

"The luncheon will be announced by a chime at noon. If we wait for that, and for the food to be laid out in our dining room, we should have an hour or two clear...or as clear as it's going to get."

Hathar consulted the slant of light through the leaves and said, "Reckon we've got an hour or more to wait then. Might as well put that time to good use." He pressed his thigh between Elin's legs with definite intent and went to work with his mouth on Elin's tender throat.

A WHILE LATER, a little disheveled from their judicious use of time, Hathar and Elin made their way back toward the palace at the sound of the chime. Inside the residence, the lunch dishes had already been laid out, and only a couple of men were seated in the dayroom, playing cards.

"You're missing it!" Hathar called to them gamely as he and Elin entered the room. "Kiran's getting trounced out there. Looks like Salin might be the new champion wrestler of the cohort!"

At that, the card players dashed outside to witness the upset.

"Can't ask for a better opening than that," Hathar said, and dragged Elin through the now unwatched service door.

The corridor beyond was different than Elin had imagined. In his mind it was dark and unkempt, full of cobwebs and dank shadows. The reality was an entirely unremarkable hallway lit by occasional narrow windows. There was a level landing to accommodate the doors, after which broad steps curved down and away, presumably to the kitchen and laundry and other unglamorous but necessary parts of the palace.

"Shall we?" Hathar said quietly, with a grand gesture down the stairs.

They crept along, careful not to make any noise, but not meeting anyone along the way. After descending what must have been about one story, there was another landing, which stretched both in front of and back past the steps. The nearest door, when cracked, showed that they were behind the baths, and Elin speculated that the other doors would lead to the residence of the raucous thirty-seventh cohort who lived below the thirty-sixth. They were the ten- to nineteen-year-olds who would only recently have been called into The Dragon's service.

"The baths are on the lower level between the residential wings, so if we can just keep heading in this direction and find a way to go back up, we should be on the right track," Elin whispered.

Pressing on again, they began to make out the occasional clatter of pots and dishes from below, and the windows fell away as the stairs passed below ground, replaced instead by lanterns set into niches carved in the stone.

The kitchen noises grew louder and more constant as they approached, making it quite clear that the room would be occupied by a number of people. By silent agreement, both men slowed their pace to creep along the wall, uncertain how, or in what direction, the passage would open up onto the kitchen.

Ahead, a change in the quality of the light indicated an opening. Elin gestured for Hathar to hang back and tiptoed up to where he could get a clear view.

They were in luck. The passage didn't require them to walk directly through the kitchen to continue. Instead, it passed a wide archway, open to the kitchen beyond. They would still need to travel a good ten feet past a dozen people, but they were all intent on their work, so it should be possible with careful timing.

Elin beckoned for Hathar to join him just at the cusp of the opening and watched for their chance. Most of the staff had their backs to the arch or were side-on and distracted, but one in particular was facing almost directly at their path, working at a high table to peel the papery skins from a mountain of garlic. It seemed as if they might be stuck there forever, as the garlic peeler stared out into space, picking halfheartedly at his monotonous task.

Finally, he huffed and got up from where he sat, brushing his hands on his apron, and wandered off to complain to a comrade who was engaged in scraping out a large ceramic pot.

Seeing an opening, Elin grabbed Hathar's hand and dashed across the archway to the other side.

They paused when just out of sight, breathing heavily but silently, and waited for any sign that they'd been seen. None came.

The corridor ahead seemed to be the mirror image of the one behind, curving upward now, with a hint of natural light filtering down from above. They came to a landing like the one behind the baths and continued up the stairs, finally arriving at what had to be the landing behind The Dragon's own chambers on the upper level of the northwest wing.

Elin's heart was pounding now. So far, this little adventure had felt like a lark, a naughty jaunt they could easily talk their way out of if pressed. Standing with only a door between him and the site of one of his most terrifying and embarrassing moments, coupled with the knowledge that what he intended to do next could easily get him booted from the haram, nearly paralyzed him.

As if sensing his trepidation, Hathar slid up behind him and wrapped his heavy arms around Elin's slight shoulders to offer a gentle squeeze. Elin was able to breathe then, grounding himself in the warm press of Hathar's body.

"Which door?" Hathar whispered. There were three laid out before them.

Elin thought about it, trying to remember his long-ago visit. "Not the first one. I can't remember if there was another room beyond her bedchamber or not. We might have to check both."

Hathar released him then, planting a kiss on his temple as he went, and approached the second door.

He listened at it first, pressing his ear intently against the wood, and, feeling a little useless, Elin went to do the same at the door further down.

He didn't hear anything, so he pressed at the door without waiting for Hathar to join him, worried his fear might get the better of him if he hesitated.

It opened smoothly, just a crack at first, but when he saw that the room was dim and no one immediately screamed to alert the guards to his presence, he opened it a little wider and slid through. This was it. The scent of the room—musk and incense masking an undeniable hint of sex, overlaid on an alien, dusty, reptilian note—took him back to that night. The shadows were different, there was no fire in the grate to bathe everything in a ruddy glow, but the room was certainly the same.

He'd taken a few hesitant steps toward the bed when it occurred to him to make sure Hathar knew they'd found the right place. He returned to the door and leaned back through. Hathar was still at the second door, just closing it behind him.

"It's this one," Elin whispered, and Hathar nodded his acknowledgment and headed his way.

"It's almost eerie. Like stepping into a memory." He was whispering directly into Hathar's ear now, standing in the doorway.

"You doing okay?" Hathar asked, searching Elin's eyes as if he might find the answer written there.

"Fine. It's odd, but not frightening. The scary part was when I didn't know what we were going to find."

He started to slip back into the room so that Hathar could follow behind him when there was a sound at the main door of the chamber, and it began to open.

In a panic, with no time to consider, Elin slammed the service door behind him, shutting Hathar out in the corridor. Simultaneously, the other door flew wide.

It was The Dragon, her expression burning with urgency teetering on the brink of rage.

Elin expected his heart to stop, or his bowels to hit the floor, but instead, his entire consciousness focused itself on the need to protect Hathar. The Dragon's face softened, her reptilian eyes dilating as she took him in, and he immediately began calculating his best chances to escape unscathed.

She had closed the door behind her and was approaching him now.

"Well hello treasure," she said with cloying sweetness, as she came within reach and stroked his cheek. She squinted slightly. "How can it be that I don't recall such a beautiful face?"

"You're to be forgiven, I'm sure. It's been years," he replied.

"Years?" Her carefully shaped brows drew together, resulting in a single wrinkle in her otherwise unblemished face. She took his chin in her hand and turned it a little, as if getting a different angle might refresh her memory.

"Yes," he said, shifting slightly to free himself from her touch. "Actually, that's sort of the reason for my visit. I hope you'll forgive me, I just didn't know how else to arrange an audience with you when you didn't want to see me." He had no idea what he was saying, but some part of him clearly had a plan, so he tried to breathe and just let the words come forth.

"I didn't want to—? Oh!" Recognition blossomed behind her eyes. "It's you."

"Yes, it's me. And...and I don't blame you for barring me from your presence after what happened. It was awful, and disgusting, and I'm sure even offensive to your god. But the fact is, I've had a sort of epiphany recently, and I just really, really needed to apologize."

She was watching him curiously now. There was no menace there, but the earlier purring intimacy was gone. "What sort of epiphany?" she asked, cocking her head in a way he found disconcertingly reminiscent of the goshawks who would occasionally land to tear apart their prey on top of the garden walls.

"Well, you see—" he took a deep breath "—I didn't really understand the meaning of your faith then—the power of Helcamet. I was young and inexperienced and too full of fear to really absorb what you were willing to teach me. I thought, for a long time, that the things you did in worship were terrifying and grotesque." He could see her curiosity edging back toward potential rage, and hurried on.

"But, *but*, I've finally taken a lover. I've found someone who has revealed to me the secrets of Helcamet, and I get it now, it all makes sense, and I feel sick that I disrespected and defiled you as I did so many years ago.

"I just wanted to say I'm sorry, and I pray that some day you'll be able to forgive me." He gazed at her expectantly, hoping his face expressed the proper combination of hope and remorse.

It seemed to work, because after a long look, she approached him again, this time to run her hands lasciviously down his chest. She leaned in close to purr in his ear, "A lover, eh? Delightful. What a lucky, lucky *dahabi.*" With her last words, she reached down to cup Elin's package and give it a possessive squeeze.

He went ice cold as every blood vessel in his body contracted at once, and he thought for sure he was going to either faint or be sick again. Somehow though, he managed to retain his grip on both consciousness and his stomach until she released him with a pat on the thigh.

As he stared at the floor, Elin tried to hide his relief behind what, with luck, would be interpreted as a suitably modest blush, all the while screaming internally for this to be over.

"I would dearly love to continue this conversation, but as it happens, I only came dashing up here because my amulet alerted me that someone other than the staff was in my chambers." She held out a translucent gray stone on a silken cord that was pulsing with an insistent violet light. "I still have a hall full of honored guests to entertain, so I really must be getting back.

"I'll arrange to make time for you soon though. You *and* your delectable lover." She was practically salivating. "I have *so* much to thank him for."

She leaned in to give Elin a lingering kiss, full of longing. "What hymns we'll sing to Helcamet," she whispered. And then she turned abruptly for the door, calling over her shoulder, "You can see yourself out the way you came in."

Elin doubled over, panting, as soon as soon as she'd left. His heart felt as if it would beat its way out of his chest. How had he survived that?

Before he knew what was happening, Hathar had entered the room and was guiding him carefully back into the passageway. As the door closed behind them, Hathar engulfed him in a warming hug, his body soothing and supporting, so he didn't even have to hold his own weight. He realized he was slick with an icy sweat, and his vision felt as if it was playing tricks on him.

"Are you all right?" Hathar asked urgently.

Elin had to take a few deep breaths, but finally worked out, "Yeah. Yes, I'm fine. She didn't do anything, I just…"

"I know," Hathar said and stood there in patient silence, stroking Elin's back as he caught his breath.

Finally, after a few minutes to collect himself, Elin said, "Let's get out of here," and headed back down the corridor, still clinging to one of Hathar's powerful hands.

The return trip was uneventful. The kitchen had quieted down, and there were only a couple of scullery maids there to be avoided. On the landing outside their quarters, they paused to listen and heard nothing. Hathar cracked the door cautiously to find no one in sight, but when they finally entered the room, Neril was there, reading in a corner that had been blocked from view.

He sneered at them. "It's not enough that you're always out fucking in the garden, now you're bothering the staff with it too?" It seemed he thought they'd been using the service corridor for a romantic tryst.

Fine, Elin thought, dragging Hathar quickly through the room and outside into the fresh air and daylight.

SAFELY SECLUDED IN the comforting embrace of the greenery around the fountain, Elin was finally able to relax. He sat on the ground between Hathar's legs and allowed his body to go limp against the reassuringly solid chest.

"I'm sorry," he finally said with a sigh.

"Sorry?" Hathar placed a cluster of kisses on the top of his head. "What for? You got us where we wanted to go and kept both our hides out of trouble. That was some damned impressive quick thinking there."

"But you didn't even get to look for the treasure. I should have waited for you to catch up with me before I opened the door; then we would have had time."

He felt Hathar shaking his head behind him.

"It's no use thinking like that. Neither of us knew there'd be an alarm. We'd both have gotten caught that way, and without nearly such a good explanation.

"Besides...there's no treasure."

Elin turned to try to look at him over his shoulder. "How can you know that? We didn't even get to check."

Hathar chuckled dryly. "Did you hear what she called you, when she walked into the room?"

Elin tried to recall, but the whole interaction was cloaked by a misty haze in his memory. "I guess not."

Hathar laced his fingers through Elin's and wrapped their arms together. "She called you 'treasure.' *You* are the treasure. Me too, I guess. The *dahabi*. Damned song was even more literal than I gave it credit for, though I guess what she does atop them by night isn't exactly sleeping."

"Oh." Elin wasn't sure what else to say.

"But hey! At least this means I have a chance of returning to my ship with a bit of the fabled hoard of Minal'taneen after all."

Hathar rocked Elin a bit, seemingly to lighten the mood, but Elin was fully occupied with deciphering his meaning. He felt a warm, tingling flush of joy as he confirmed for himself that yes, Hathar had just implied— But Hathar was going on, and seemed to want Elin's full attention.

"Aaand, speaking of... Did you happen to notice the mirror on The Dragon's chamber wall?"

Elin took a moment to consult his memory. There had been a mirror there, but it hadn't seemed particularly interesting to him. It hung in a large ornate frame on the northwest wall of the room, positioned to neatly reflect The Dragon's bed. He didn't really want to spend too much time with the idea of what that mirror was intended for.

"Yes, I suppose I did. At least, I saw there was a mirror. What of it?"

"And what about outside?" Hathar asked, dropping the matter of the mirror for the moment. "Have you ever noticed how the mountain stone is worked right into the structure of the palace?"

Elin felt he was losing the thread now.

"I...guess I have? Makes a strong foundation, right?"

"Oh, I'm sure of it. Very sound. Very sensible. Especially where it reaches all the way up to buttress the northwest wing—all the way up to the second floor, to just about exactly where that mirror is hanging, if I'm not mistaken."

"Are you saying...? I'm not sure what you're saying. You think there's something behind the mirror?" Elin sat up and turned to face Hathar, hoping to learn more from his expression.

"I'm saying that powerful people sometimes get in trouble with other powerful people, and, that being the case, they like to build their homes with a plan B in mind."

Hathar looked at him meaningfully, giving the information a moment to settle in.

"You think there's a hidden passage behind the mirror."

"I do."

Elin's head swam at the notion that their escape could be so close, so simple.

"But she has that amulet. She'll know if we go back. I don't think we can get away with using the service corridors a second time."

"Ah, but we won't have to." The familiar twinkle was there in Hathar's eyes, but tinged with something else. Concern? Wariness? "The Dragon's taken a renewed personal interest in you and your 'delectable lover,' remember? She's almost certainly going to grace us with an invitation to her chambers any time now."

Elin had forgotten about that, but now it was rushing back, the purr of her voice and her hand on his crotch and a promise of, "hymns to Helcamet," and he felt his pulse quicken and his head grow light.

"Hey! Hey!" Hathar was saying, his hands firm on Elin's shoulders. "Stick with me here." Elin realized from the look of concern on Hathar's face how close he must have been to losing consciousness. "We're not going to let anything happen in there. We're just going to use it as our opening to get out of this damned place."

We.

Elin clung to that word and then leaned forward to cling to Hathar. It would be all right. Whatever happened next, they would face it together.

Chapter Eight

IT WAS NIGHT, and Hathar and Elin were tucked away in their alcove off the bedchamber. Elin couldn't sleep, though he'd been trying to lose himself in the rhythm of Hathar's steady breathing for what felt like an hour. His thoughts were racing.

Finally, he whispered, "Hathar."

No reply.

He tried again, this time adding a gentle nip on Hathar's shoulder where it was within reach.

That, it seemed, was enough, as Hathar grumbled and rolled blearily toward him, muttering, "What?"

"This afternoon, with The Dragon… I was mostly saying whatever it seemed like I had to—to protect you and get out of there. But I did mean what I said about what you've done for me."

Hathar's eyes were open now, if only partially, so Elin went on, still whispering to avoid waking the others.

"I don't think I'll ever be the type to sing hymns to Helcamet, but the way I feel with you, if that's how The Dragon feels with all of her *dahabi*, I can see how you could base a religion on that feeling."

Elin took a deep breath and stared up at the ceiling. "I guess I just wanted to make sure you knew that. But also, even though I feel that way, I know you've had a whole life before this, and it's waiting for you to pick it back up as soon as you leave, and we haven't really talked about how or if I might fit there.

"I know I probably seem naive, but I've read just about every story in the library. I know that what might seem like a brilliant diversion in limited circumstances can lose its shine when those limitations are released. If you don't think..." He scrunched his eyes shut tight for a moment before relaxing, trying to keep his emotions under control. "If I should stay here, I will. You can tell me. I'll still help you escape. I just don't—" He took a ragged breath, afraid his voice would betray him if he tried to continue.

Hathar was fully awake now, and he lay on his side gazing fixedly at Elin. Elin was still staring upward, avoiding the need to look at him. When Hathar reached out to give a tentative stroke to his arm, Elin grimaced in response.

"Hey," Hathar said softly, sliding closer to wrap himself around the still-rigid Elin. "I'm sorry. I guess I should have said something a while ago, but it felt like it was obvious." He kissed Elin's shoulder and cheek, pausing for a moment as if considering his next words.

"You're right. I've had a whole life before this. Let's be genteel and say that, in bedroom matters, I am anything *but* naive.

"I've had friends, I've had lovers, but what I haven't had is this...*thing* that I feel with you. The first time I saw you, outside the baths, it was like I already knew you. Like your face was already in my memory, even though we'd never met. I tried to dismiss it, pretend it was just run of the mill attraction, but the closer I got to you, the stronger it became.

"I can't imagine not having you beside me now. What would I do without your beautiful spirit, your bravery? That place that came reserved for you in my mind would feel like an empty, sucking hole without you there."

Elin turned a little to look at him, still keeping a tight rein on his emotions so that he could take in every word. Hathar's expression, picked out in chiaroscuro by the moonlight from the high window, spoke of intense sincerity—a striking counterpoint to his usual cavalier smirk.

"When I took that minstrel on board, I was right to think he might bring me good fortune. I don't want to even consider a reality where I didn't hear that song—didn't come here to find you. You *are* a treasure, and I would be honored if you would agree to sail by my side."

One tear escaped from the corner of Elin's eye, but he was smiling now. Beaming, actually. He leaned over impulsively and caught Hathar's lips in an urgent kiss.

The kiss slowed and deepened and Elin ground against Hathar with clear, lascivious intent.

"I'd have spoken up a lot sooner if I'd known it would get me this kind of reaction." Hathar chuckled.

Elin's only reply was a husky, "Maybe we should move to the other room."

Not needing to be asked twice, Hathar untangled himself from Elin and the bedclothes to stand, reaching back to offer a hand up. They crept through the door into the adjoining chamber and headed for the oversized upholstered seat they favored.

Elin got there first and pulled Hathar down on top of him, relishing the solid weight of Hathar's ropy body. He picked up the kiss where they'd left off, hands roaming, trying to take in every inch of his lover, every cleft and plane, as their tongues danced.

Things went on this way, their passion building, their cocks erect and aimlessly clashing together with just enough friction to both tantalize and frustrate, until Elin broke off and whispered, "I want to try something."

Hathar raised an eyebrow and gave Elin's nipple a playful tweak as he replied, "Anything, my sweet. What do you have in mind?"

A little of his earlier urgency seemed to dissipate as Elin struggled with the next words. "Well...you know that statue in the garden? The one with the two men, face to face, but you can see that one is..." He trailed off for a moment, a little shy of the words. "I want to see what it would be like to have you inside me."

Hathar looked overcome by lust to hear those words from Elin's lips, but his expression was tempered by a tiny wrinkle of concern.

"Are you sure?"

Elin nodded in response and said softly, "When we go before The Dragon, I want to go in knowing that anything she can ask of me, I've already had with you. I want to be able to armor myself with the memory of your touch."

Hathar drew him close and squeezed until Elin's bones creaked. "Let's armor you then."

He released Elin gently back onto the seat, and then, kissing him lightly, stood and walked toward the bedchamber. The soft creak of the door came to Elin from where he lay, followed by some muffled rustling and another creak, and Hathar was back again.

He knelt over Elin, bending low for another kiss to stoke the fires, and trailed his lips down over

Elin's chest and stomach to nibble briefly at the crease of his thigh. Elin squirmed at the faintly ticklish sensation, and Hathar shifted his attention to give a few leisurely sucks to his cock, bathing it in slippery spit. He used his hand to take over for his mouth and proceeded to kiss and lick his way further south, anointing Elin's balls, and onward between his legs until he arrived at the edge of Elin's tender bud.

Still pumping Elin's cock in a gentle rhythm, Hathar swirled his tongue in a single circle over the puckered flesh.

Elin gasped, and bucked, clearly with pleasure rather than alarm. "Did you just—?" he choked out, wonder in his voice.

"Mmmhmm," was Hathar's only reply, and the vibration of his low murmur on Elin's most sensitive parts introduced yet another layer of sensation.

Hathar lapped at his entrance again, his touch growing firmer and more insistent, matched by the work of his hand. Elin hadn't expected this. He'd hoped it would be good, of course, but no amount of imagining could have prepared him for the heady cocktail of feeling so completely vulnerable and exposed, but simultaneously worshiped.

Instinctively, he drew his knees up near his shoulders to grant Hathar better access, which was all the encouragement Hathar required to finally broach the tight ring with the tip of his tongue. Elin sighed in response, melting into the wet intimacy of Hathar's mouth on his ass.

With Elin's hole moist and pliant, Hathar put two fingers into his mouth before returning it to work on Elin's now-throbbing erection. He bobbed and sucked, at the same time working first one finger, and then two, inside Elin. This stretching skirted the edge of pain, but when Hathar hooked his fingers in a gentle beckoning motion, any discomfort was forgotten. Elin choked back a shout and, panting, managed, "Please. I don't think I can last!"

With a few parting thrusts, Hathar gently withdrew his fingers and slid himself up to place a smoldering kiss on Elin's lips. He sat up then, leaning back to reach something on the floor, and Elin heard the sound of a corked bottle being opened. His mouth went dry at the sight of Hathar looming over him in the dim moonlight, his rippling muscles picked out in silver, cock gleaming as he stroked it with oil. A shiver rippled through Elin as he entertained the thought that all of that, within and without, was for him.

Hathar leaned down and eased Elin's knees up from where they'd relaxed during the interlude. He ran his oil-slick cock up and down the cleft a few times, finally aligning his head with Elin's entrance. "Try to open up for me," he whispered, applying a slight pressure. Elin did as he was asked, eager to be filled again, though well aware that Hathar's rod had a lot more girth than two fingers.

It seemed, for a moment, as if penetration would be impossible, but when Hathar ran his fingertips tenderly down Elin's ribs he writhed, relaxing and driving himself onto Hathar, inviting him in.

As Hathar's first few inches slid past the tight ring, Elin tensed, overwhelmed by the intensity. He willed himself to relax again, focusing on the thrill of having Hathar *inside* him, and his desire to take him fully. As Elin adjusted, Hathar drew out a little and then slid back in, and that tiny motion completely changed the character of the sensation to one of pure pleasure. Elin moaned and rolled his hips, encouraging Hathar to continue.

With each painstaking stroke, Hathar drove a little deeper until he was completely buried in Elin's snug warmth, sending showers of electric sparks through Elin with every pass.

As the pace increased, Elin lost track of his body, his whole existence reduced to a throbbing epicenter of pleasure. He began to yelp and make unintelligible noises as the more sophisticated portions of his brain checked out at the onslaught.

Just as Elin thought he couldn't possibly take any more, Hathar brought a hand between them and wrapped it firmly around Elin's cock, pumping in time to his penetration. With only a few strokes, Elin began to lose the thread of reality, his consciousness consumed by shuddering waves ripping through his body.

Hathar was clearly teetering on the brink. Presented with his lover contorted with pleasure and lying completely exposed beneath him, he groaned and gave a last great thrust, filling Elin with his seed and collapsing to rest on top of him.

They both lay in silence for several minutes, allowing their brains to sift back into some semblance of order and their bodies likewise.

Finally, Elin breathed out an awestruck, "Fuck..."

Hathar's body shook with mirth, and he muttered thickly into the upholstery, "I thought that was my line."

"That was just..." Elin trailed off again, and finally settled for "Thank you" as it became apparent nothing more eloquent was going to present itself in his current state.

He may have drifted off for a while then, because the next thing he knew, Hathar was heaving him up off the seat and dragging him in the direction of the bedchamber.

"Come love, let's get to our proper bed," he was saying. "We might need our beauty sleep. Could be a big day tomorrow."

THEY SLEPT LONG and hard, and the room was fully lit with late morning sunlight when Elin finally cracked his eyelids. As he stretched, a smattering of little aches and pains brought the events of the night before rushing back. His heart gave an extra beat and a grin spread across his face.

He yawned and rolled to one side. Hathar was still asleep, and Elin took a moment to bask in his hawkish profile, the slight bristle of stubble that seemed to grace his chin no matter how recently he'd shaved, the silky sweep of his white-gold hair. He was still in awe that all this was his for the taking.

As if in response to his gaze, Hathar smiled, his eyes still closed. "Ready to face the day?" he asked.

"Ready if you are," Elin replied, sitting up with a groan.

The other beds were empty, and the sounds of breakfast were filtering in from the adjoining rooms. They rose and threw on clothes before wandering, still a little groggy, into the dining room.

Elin didn't feel quite ready to eat and was just savoring the aroma of his coffee in anticipation of that first fortifying sip as Emun approached the table. He looked like he was barely able to contain his excitement as he waited to be acknowledged.

Hathar was focused on filling his mouth from the mound of food already on his plate, so it fell to Elin to deal with the guard.

"Go ahead," he said, terse before his coffee had a chance to set in.

Emun beamed and leaned in close, resting his hands on the table. "I've got some pretty unexpected news for you!" he said, his eyes bright. Elin's stomach clenched in anticipation of the only "unexpected news" that would have the staff acting so giddy. He knew he should try to appear at least mildly interested, but just didn't have it in him.

Hathar spared him, breaking in with a brusque, "What is it then?"

"Weeell..." Emun seemed little deterred by the unenthusiastic reception, his voice still rich with relish over juicy gossip. "You're being summoned to The Dragon's chambers. Both of you. Tonight!" He gave them a meaningful look, clearly waiting for a reaction.

"Fine," Hathar said, returning to his meal.

That did take the wind out of Emun's sails a bit. He turned to Elin.

"You must be thrilled." He pressed. "This could really turn things around for you! Give her what she's looking for, and this could be the start of a whole new chapter."

"Yes." Elin replied flatly. "Thank you. We'll be ready at the usual time."

Emun was clearly perplexed by their lack of excitement, but he knew when he was being dismissed and dutifully excused himself back to his post near the wall.

Elin closed his eyes and blew out a breath, still cradling his undrunk coffee.

Hathar dished up a second plate and slid it over to rest between Elin's elbows. "Eat up," he ordered. "You're going to need your strength."

BACK IN THE garden, Elin was pacing.

"I thought we'd have more time than this." He ran his hands over his face, rubbing his eyes. "It's what, almost noon? We'll be sent for at seven, and we need to bathe and dress before then, so we've got...six hours to plan a brilliant and daring escape."

He crumpled to the ground, legs folded to his chest. "This isn't going to work." Leaning against the edge of the fountain, he dropped his head to his knees.

Hathar came to sit on the ledge of the fountain next to him and squeezed his shoulder with a steady hand. "I can come up with all kinds of brilliant and daring in six hours. It's going to be fine."

Elin didn't seem to hear, instead musing aloud, "I guess we can just go through with it... If we perform, give her what she wants, she should be worn out after, right? We can wait for her to fall asleep and then go for the mirror and just pray you're right about there being a passage." He sighed.

Hathar grew stern. "No. That is not plan A. We're not going to fuck her. *You're* definitely not. You almost blacked out remembering her touch. There's no way I'm sitting there on silken sheets pretending to serve her royal scaliness while you're suffering. We can do better."

"How!?" Elin spread his hands in a pleading gesture and turned to stare at Hathar, eyes wide.

Hathar slid to the ground, wrapped an arm around Elin, and pulled him over to lean against his shoulder. "Well, I've been thinking."

Elin peered at him out of the corner of his eye with curious skepticism.

"I was thinking about what you said, how there's no gold or metal at all in the kingdom. It's a nice story— The Dragon's religious devotion, swearing off the things that dragons are supposed to prize the most so she can focus on her, uh...*offerings* to Helcamet, but I think there might be something more to it. Or even if there isn't, at this point she hasn't touched gold in, what? Four hundred years? The stuff is supposed to drive dragons crazy under normal circumstances, but now she's...sensitized, right? Craving it.

"So, in her chamber, I can present her with a token of my esteem—a golden ring! If it doesn't do anything, then okay, maybe we have to default to your plan, or more likely, I'll just have to kill her."

Elin sat up at that. "You can't! I mean, I'm pretty sure you actually can't. She may look like a human woman, but she really is a dragon. But beyond that, what would happen to everyone else here with her gone? What they have isn't perfect, but it's all they have. I want to do this, but not at the expense of everyone I've ever known. They may be intolerable, but they still don't deserve that. If it comes to it, I'll do what she asks. I'll do that for you—but no killing."

Hathar took a moment to absorb that. Finally, he drew a deep breath. "All right. Anyway, what I'm hoping is that the gold will create some kind of distraction. She might get...hypnotized by it, or knock a wall down, or storm out in a rage— I don't know, but I'm sure, *sure* that there's a passage out of the palace behind that mirror, and we'll use the distraction to take our chance to find it and get out of here."

After a pause, Elin said, "That's...leaving a lot up to luck."

Hathar shrugged. "I've done a lot of my best work that way. It's not like she's going to sit down to give me tips on how to subdue her and stage an escape. I have to do what I can to stack the deck in our favor and go for it."

They sat in uneasy silence as Elin searched his mind for a useful objection or a better alternative, but came up empty. His brow furrowed, Elin cocked his head at Hathar. "Uh...one thing. Where are you going to get this gold ring? The whole plan is based on the idea that there's no metal in the kingdom, right?"

That was met with a smirk as Hathar heaved himself off the ground and started to undo his trousers.

Elin's eyebrows crept practically up to his hairline at this development, and he shook his head slightly. "Is this an answer to my question, or are you just trying to distract me?"

Rather than reply, Hathar simply finished with the ties and stripped down to his knees. As Elin gaped, he lifted his flaccid member to reveal an intricately engraved ring, worked right through the skin at the top of his scrotum. It was placed so as to be practically invisible under normal circumstances, but now glinted alluringly over the sandy hair and tender pink flesh.

Elin reached out a finger to explore the place where the ring ran through the skin, and Hathar's sensitive sack roiled at the contact. Several questions warred in his mind, and came out as a spluttering, "What?"

Hathar grinned and fingered the ring a little himself. "Had it done years ago, on an island where we happened to stop over on a spice run. The people there had rings through everything. I thought it could come in handy some day, a little gold where no one would think to look. Plus it's kinda sexy, right?" He raised an eyebrow devilishly.

Elin pulled himself up to sit on the edge of the fountain, putting his face even with Hathar's crotch, and leaned in to get a better look. He'd never seen gold, or any metal, before. It shone more richly, mellower than polished glass, but far smoother than even the finest woodwork. The way it lay against the skin suggested a fair amount of weight for its size. He could see now that the engraving depicted a stylized dragon, its serpentine body passing through the skin, front and rear legs meeting to clasp a golden ball.

He kissed it reverently and bathed the surrounding tissue with his tongue. Hathar gave a moan of appreciation as his head lolled back.

Elin ran his hands softly up Hathar's inner thighs and cupped his sack from behind, teasing the perineum with a couple of fingers. With his free hand he gripped the base of Hathar's rapidly hardening cock and guided the head to his mouth.

He nibbled the delicate edge of Hathar's foreskin and slid it back to taste the unprotected glans, pumping idly at the lower part of the shaft. He roamed over Hathar's heavy balls with his other hand, spreading and playing in the slick saliva he'd left there.

Absurd that in such a short time these acts had come to feel like going home. Was he really the same man who less than two weeks ago recoiled from even the thought of such intimacies? He was, of course, and could confirm it by imagining anyone other than Hathar on the receiving end of his attentions and feeling a trace of the old panic rise. Somehow, chance had brought him the only person he'd ever met who made him feel right in his thoughts and valued for more than just a fluke of his birth, who opened his mind to possibilities beyond the palace walls. That rightness freed him to explore, for the first time, his own sensuality and the dizzying power of pleasuring another. He wouldn't let it go—not now, not ever, even if he had to subject himself to The Dragon to keep it.

Chapter Nine

SEVEN O'CLOCK ARRIVED finding Elin and Hathar waiting nervously just inside their residence door, bathed and dressed for their audience with The Dragon. Hathar had removed the ring, with Elin's assistance, and stowed it in his pocket to be presented at an opportune moment.

The door swung open and an unfamiliar guard entered, brimming with the same irritating jollity that had infected Emun that morning.

"Big night, eh, boys?" he offered, seeming to only barely restrain himself from nudging Hathar with a friendly elbow in the ribs.

"If we play our cards right," was Hathar's somewhat more subdued reply, but if the guard noticed they didn't quite seem to share his enthusiasm, he didn't let on.

The guard guided them through the door and off to the right, following the familiar path down the corridor to the stairs that led to the baths below. This time though, they continued on along a similar corridor until it was cut off by a set of heavy double doors flanked by a pair of significantly less jovial guards.

Their guide exchanged nods with the sentinels, and the door was opened for them. Beyond, the corridor continued. Paintings of The Dragon with her *dahabi*, even more explicit than those that hung in the gallery, if that was even possible, adorned the walls, and the air became heavy with incense, musk, and something else.

They passed two doors, and then the guard stopped at the third. He turned to Elin and Hathar and said, "This is it. Ready for your grand entrance?" He clapped Elin on the shoulder with a good-natured exuberance that almost tipped him off balance, and turned to rap smartly on the door.

As they waited, Elin took Hathar's hand and brought it to his mouth for a kiss. Hathar turned and planted a much more fervent kiss on Elin's lips in response.

Elin thought he caught the guard eyeing them, but his attention was diverted when a soft voice from beyond the door called, "Bring them in."

The guard opened the door then and stood back to allow Hathar and Elin to enter.

The chamber was just as it had been the day before, with the exception of a fire in the grate and The Dragon wearing considerably less clothing. She was standing with causal elegance, one arm on the mantel, as if posed. Her negligee left little to the imagination, the gauzy material plunging low between her breasts and slit high over her thighs.

"Thank you," she said, and the guard backed through the door, shutting it as he went.

She approached, saying, "Please, make yourselves comfortable," and gesturing to the extravagantly large four-poster bed.

They seated themselves as indicated, Hathar managing to recline in a sprawling unconcerned fashion, Elin rather more upright, with his legs tucked under him.

The Dragon joined them, perching herself on Hathar's knee and plunging her fingers delightedly into his hair. "Platinum!" she cried. "My late bloomer has exotic tastes!"

Hathar tipped his head back, almost seeming to enjoy the attention. Elin felt something hard and ugly start to rise in his throat, but he swallowed it down, assuring himself this was an act for The Dragon's benefit. As long as Hathar stayed the focus, Elin would be relatively safe, and he was thankful for that.

"Of course, I've been meaning to have you up to my chamber since I heard you'd been found," The Dragon was saying. "It's not every day that we get such an unusual new addition. I do have so many *dahabi* though"—there was a faraway gleam in her eye as she seemed to be envisioning the scope of her hoard—"and I really owe my attention to all of them. I just hadn't managed to find the time!"

She still had one hand in Hathar's hair, but the other was now roaming over his chest and arms, fondling his biceps and teasing at his nipples.

"But when our lovely one here"—she gave a meaningful glance at Elin—"came to tell me of his lover, and I learned that lover was you, I knew it was well past time for a meeting."

Her use of "our" sat in Elin's stomach like a stone, but he remained impassive.

Hathar had a hand on her bare thigh now, and when he stroked it, and she let out an indulgent little moan, Elin had to get away. He stood, trying to feign a casual interest in the carvings on the mantelpiece: a series of particularly flexible men and women chained in an arrangement of reciprocal pleasure.

Elin's back was to them when he heard Hathar say, "Oh, before I forget!"

Elin turned slightly to bring the scene into his peripheral vision as The Dragon crooned, "What is it?"

"Nothing much, your majesty, but if you'd do me the favor of letting me up, I've brought you a token of thanks for welcoming me so graciously into your household."

Elin wandered toward the mirror, pretending to examine his reflection but instead watching intently as Hathar stood and then settled The Dragon onto the edge of the mattress where he'd been sitting only a few seconds before. She gazed at him with expectant curiosity as he knelt at her feet and took her hand.

"You've welcomed a ragged stranger into your palace and conferred on him all the luxuries of royalty. Without your generosity, I would never have met the person with whom I feel the most at home, the piece of myself I didn't know was missing. I hope this token will in some small way express the gratitude I owe to you."

With that, Hathar reached into his pocket and drew out the ring, and then slipped it deftly over The Dragon's slender finger.

For a long moment, nothing happened. She stared fixedly at her hand, almost as if in a trance.

Hathar glanced up and caught Elin's eye in the mirror. They shared a look of uncertainty as they waited to see if her state would persist, or if something more would happen.

Slowly, she brought her other hand up to clutch her finger where the ring encircled it, still gazing raptly at the gold. "I..." she began, and trailed off.

With The Dragon distracted, Elin began to discreetly run his fingers along the edge of the mirror frame, seeking a latch or a hinge or some mechanism that might hint at how to access the passage they hoped was hidden behind.

Meanwhile, Hathar still knelt at The Dragon's feet, his focus on her face as if it might offer some clue as to what would happen next. She might be permanently incapacitated or only momentarily stunned, and a miscalculation could doom them both.

She tried to speak again. "It's very..." A look of mild concern crossed her face, and one of her elegantly arched eyebrows elongated itself into a waving tendril for a second, snapping back into place only as her lips tightened in concentration.

"Your majesty?" Hathar prompted.

She started to speak again, but before she managed to form a word, she was caught in a sputtering cough, a flurry of sparks erupting from her lips and extinguishing themselves before they hit the floor.

His eyes widened in shock, but he seemed to steel himself against his own reaction, backing away only slightly as a long, serpentine tail unleashed itself from her negligee. Both eyebrows were tendrils now, refusing to be contained.

Suddenly, with a strange roar that started as a human scream of frustration, the beautiful woman before him was transfigured into a massive scaled dragon, her many coils crimped and bound by the stout posts and canopy of the bed.

Hathar leapt up and ran to join Elin at the mirror, throwing it off the wall as The Dragon struggled to free herself from the bedframe and its voluminous hangings. A crash of shattering glass was added to the chaos in the room, and the passage they'd been counting on was revealed as a rough opening in the stone wall.

They barreled through, running as fast as they could into the swiftly increasing darkness, the sounds of The Dragon's struggle still far too close behind them.

'We should've brought a fucking light!" Hathar yelled, but they continued as quickly as they could through the inky black, thankful at least that the narrowness of the passage made it easy to follow.

They pressed on like that, blind but for the cues from their fingers on the rough-hewn stone, for a period of time that felt almost endless, but was in reality a mere ten or fifteen minutes. At that point, the passage stopped, dead-ending in a wall of even more stone.

"This can't be," Hathar whispered urgently. "You don't build a tunnel like this and then stop before you get anywhere useful."

Elin's pulse was racing from both exertion and panic as he frantically ran his fingers over the walls again and again, hoping to find an opening he'd somehow missed.

The stone of the wall blocking their progress was different from the stone of the tunnel walls: rougher, with more sharp angles. Elin ran his hands over it again and then said, "I think this wall is made up of stacked stones rather than carved from the earth. Maybe we could push it down?"

As he spoke, an alarming thundering sound echoed down the tunnel. The Dragon must have freed herself and was now swiftly approaching.

"We'd better try!" Hathar replied, applying his shoulder to the stone and pushing with all the force he could muster.

Elin could hear Hathar's grunt of exertion as he strained at the wall, but nothing happened.

Elin imagined them perishing here, trapped in the dark, hemmed in by stone.

"It's not coming down, but I think I felt something give a little near the top," Hathar reported. There were some directionless fumbling sounds and a scrape before a stone fell away, admitting a waft of fresh air and a narrow shaft of moonlight.

The sound of The Dragon's approach was growing more insistent.

"That hole's too small for me, but you should fit," Hathar hissed.

Before he knew what was happening, Elin was being boosted up to slither through the opening and emerge onto a desolate moonlit beach littered with huge slabs of rock that had fallen from the cliffs above.

"See if you can move any more stones from that side," Hathar called after him.

From where Elin stood, it was apparent the tunnel had been sealed from the beach side by simply piling up a mound of boulders. Most were far too large for him to hope to move, but near the top, where Hathar had found success, there were a few Elin thought he might be able to pry free.

He grabbed at the most likely one and pulled as hard as he could, coming away with nothing but a throbbing fingernail bent back past the quick.

"She's coming!" Hathar's usually confident voice was now tinged with panic as it rose up from below.

Casting around in desperation, Elin's eyes lit on a stout driftwood branch. He grabbed it and shoved it into the hole he had come through, wedging the end behind a stone and using the edge of the tunnel opening as a fulcrum. Elin brought all his weight to bear on the makeshift lever, and almost wept when the stone began to move. He heaved on until the stone popped free and rolled down over its brethren to the beach.

He threw himself to the ground and thrust an arm through the enlarged hole. Hathar had already scaled most of the wall, but he eagerly grasped Elin's offered hand and hauled himself the rest of the way up. The sound of The Dragon's approach was audible even from this side of the wall now. They would have to hope that the unexpected barrier would slow her as well.

With Hathar clear of the tunnel, both men scrambled down the pile of stones to the beach.

"What now?" Elin pleaded. "She's going to burst out of there any second."

Hathar glanced around the desolate beach. He then grabbed Elin's hand and set off toward a heap of stone slabs maybe fifty yards away.

"Climb in there," Hathar ordered, gesturing to the series of lean-tos and passages created by the boulders as they'd fallen against each other. "I'm right behind you. Just keep going until you're someplace small enough and deep enough that you don't think a dragon can reach."

Elin had no idea what a dragon could do, but he worked his way between the stones until it seemed he was buried near the center of the pile. Narrow slits between the slabs allowed a limited view of the tunnel entrance in one direction, and the sea and sky in another. He hunkered there, waiting for Hathar to catch up.

A mighty rumble emanated from the blocked tunnel opening as Hathar joined Elin in their found bunker. It would appear that The Dragon had reached the wall and was trying to batter it down with her body, shaking the hillside and sending down showers of small stones.

Every few seconds, the earth would vibrate with the impact of The Dragon's body against the blockade until, in a deafening explosion of rock and scales, she burst through, the stone collapsing and resealing the tunnel behind her.

She rose up in the air, her serpentine body undulating like a kite in the wind as she scanned the beach, and dove low to skim over the stones in search of her quarry.

Elin found Hathar's hand in the darkness and squeezed it tight, willing his breath to still and his heart to pound silently.

A shadow passed over the seaward opening to their bunker; it seemed as if she might have overlooked them. That hope was dashed by a scrabbling of claws on stone as a single reptilian eye peered in at them through the crack.

She tried to reach through the opening with her scaly talon as Hathar and Elin clung to the back wall of their refuge, but the slabs were too thick, the space too deep for her to reach them. She retreated, only to reappear to try again at the other opening with the same results.

She roared with what sounded like frustration, sending a gout of flame licking into the sky; then, with a huff of sulfurous breath, she seemed to collect herself, neatly arranging her coils and settling onto the gravel of the beach.

For a completely disorienting moment, all light and sound seemed drawn into a vacuum centered on The Dragon, before snapping suddenly back to normal as she contracted into her human form. In apparent fury, she ripped the ring from her finger and hurled it toward the sea.

"Is this what you want?" she shouted, all the purring coquetry now gone from her voice. "To be stranded on a desolate shore with no food, no provisions, savoring your precious freedom until you die of starvation or exposure?

"If I didn't treasure you, I could sear you to ash with a breath. I could knock down your childish little fortress and crush you beneath the stones. I've given you everything. We could be safe and warm in luxury, singing praises to Helcamet right now. How can you imagine this is any kind of victory?"

She stepped closer and brought her face to the crack, her tone softer.

"Like this, in my human form, I could crawl right in there with you. I could show you the true glory of Helcamet right here among the boulders and have you begging me to carry you back to the palace."

She gave them a sultry stare, as if expecting one or both to leap at the offer, but was met only with silence.

"I'm not going to do that though," she sniffed. "I'm going to leave you here to experience the consequences of your actions. When I think you've had enough time to consider, maybe I'll come back and bring you home. Or maybe I'll let you perish. New *dahabi* are being born all the time; it's not as if my haram is truly diminished by the loss of two." Her conviction seemed to waver a bit on that last point.

"Have fun!" she said, turning to go, and then paused to turn back as if remembering something.

"And don't go looking for your boat, Platinum. I've burned it."

With that, she swept back into her monstrous form and took to the sky, headed in the direction of the palace.

Chapter Ten

HATHAR COLLAPSED AGAINST Elin as The Dragon disappeared into the night.

They sat in silence, absorbing the enormity of her parting shot.

Hathar's ship, burned. His crew, his father's legacy, all lost in pursuit of a fortune that didn't exist. Their only hope for escape from this godsforsaken stretch of beach, blackened at the bottom of the sea.

"I fucking deserve this," Hathar growled at last, shoving off of Elin to press his head against the unforgiving stone. "I took this idiot gamble based on a song and a hunch and bald-faced greed, and if I lose my life and livelihood because of it, so be it. But you... Them... FUCK!"

He drove his fist into the slab where his forehead rested, seeming to welcome the pain.

"I chose to come," Elin said softly. He tried to divine any reaction from Hathar, but if there was one, it was lost in the darkness. He went on.

"I took my own gamble. A chance at real life with you over a guarantee of captive luxury. And your men... I didn't know them, but if your venture had succeeded, you'd all have been rich, right? They chose to gamble on you as their captain instead of settling for the stability of straightforward trading. We all do what we think is best."

Hathar breathed deep and lifted his head to face Elin in the dim light. There was no way to make out his expression, but his body language and the very vibrations coming off him still spoke of rage and grief. He seemed unconvinced by Elin's rationalization.

"I'm such a fool! She's a dragon, not an imbecile. I show up out of nowhere in her magically hidden seaside town, looking like absolutely no one else. Of course she knew there had to be a ship out there somewhere, and that I'd want to get back to it. Telling them to hide in the next cove over might as well have the rat hide in the terrier's kennel. She probably picked them off before they even had a chance to fight back."

Elin flinched as Hathar suddenly gave voice to a bellow that sought to vent his guilt and helplessness and pain. It rang off the walls of their tiny refuge and echoed distantly along the cliffs.

As the vibrations died away, Elin reached out to Hathar, whose fury seemed to have been transmuted through sound into something much mellower and sadder.

He rested a hand on Hathar's shoulder and said, "We'll need to mourn. You've lost things you didn't even know were at stake. Right now though"—he proceeded carefully—"at this moment, we're stranded on a beach with The Dragon liable to come back at any time. What can we do to ensure that we're not left mourning one another as well?"

This seemed to get Hathar's attention in a way nothing else had so far. He took Elin's hand, squeezed it, and said, "Let's get out of this rock pile, for a start."

They crawled out from between the stones the same way they'd crawled in, but with much less urgency, finally standing stiffly outside the heap and taking some time to stretch out the kinks that had set in while they were confined.

Elin gazed out over the beach for a moment. It would have been beautiful, really, under other circumstances. The cliffs stood high and severe, cracked into improbably perfect rectangles that created the sea of boulders at their base. Fine gravel, mostly dark like the stone, but punctuated by bits of shells and coral that echoed the pinpoint lights of the stars above, filled the gaps between the larger rocks and became predominant as the land ran down to the sea. The water glinted in the faint moonlight, scoring the scene with a gentle rhythmic murmur as it lapped at the land.

Elin crunched down the beach toward the shore where Hathar joined him, placing a weary arm around his shoulder.

"You can go back," Hathar said, staring out to sea. "I won't think less of you."

"No," was Elin's firm reply. "There's nothing there for me now, and I'd prefer never to see The Dragon again. We'll have to wait for daylight, but we can try to make our way over the cliffs." He turned around, pulling Hathar with him, to look back up at the stone wall, scanning for some sign of a path or gap. "There are people who live in the plains on the other side of the mountains. Surely we can build some kind of life among them."

"We'll have to try," Hathar agreed, eyeing the forbidding cliffs with very little optimism.

As they stood there considering their next move, the rhythm of the waves began to change, first subtly, but slowly becoming more persistent—a measured splashing overlaying the more free-form rippling near the shore.

Hathar glanced absently over his shoulder, looked again, and abruptly grabbed Elin by the arm before turning to run down the beach.

There was a rowboat there, within several yards of shore, making steady progress in their direction.

"Hoy!" Hathar shouted at the indistinct figure in the craft.

"Hallo!" came the reply.

"Rath?!" Hathar's voice was transfigured by hope, and he looked about to fall to his knees there in the damp gravel.

Elin glanced from the boat to Hathar in disbelief. "Is this one of your crew?"

Just as he asked, a call came back from the water in response to Hathar's question: "The same! Is that you cap'n?"

Hathar was wading into the sea now, rushing to meet the boat as it drew near. Elin followed a little behind, and heard a grating crunch as the craft was pulled up to rest on the shore.

The other man was almost bowled over by the intensity of Hathar's embrace as he grabbed him over the low side of the dinghy. "How can you be here?" Hathar sounded almost breathless. "The Dragon said she'd burned you all to ash." He stepped back then, granting the sailor space to come ashore.

"I don't know anything about that," he said. "We've just been at anchor waiting for your return, but the watch saw a flare in the sky here and we thought we'd better send someone to check it out, lest you were in some kind of trouble."

"Oh, we have trouble, but it's already diminished a great deal just by seeing you here!" Hathar clapped his subordinate on the shoulder.

"Let's get back to *The Prudent Mistress*. We can catch up once aboard, but I want to set sail right away. I won't rest easy until we're well clear of the Southern Sea."

Hathar suddenly seemed to remember Elin, who had been hanging back a bit and watching the reunion in a state of relieved shock. He trotted over and took his love in his arms. Gracing his lips with a brief, joyful kiss, he then dragged him down to board the little craft.

"Elin, Rath. Rath, Elin," Hathar said, making vague introductory motions. "Elin will be sailing with us from now on."

Rath might have raised an eyebrow as he pushed the dinghy off the beach and hopped aboard himself, but it was hard to tell in the dim starlight. There was definitely a hint of amusement in his voice as he asked, "So'll we need to hang another hammock, then?"

"That won't be necessary," Hathar replied with mock seriousness as he pulled Elin to huddle close to him on the bench.

DESPITE HIS EARLIER conviction that he would not rest easy until they'd cleared the Southern Sea, Hathar found himself blearily grasping at consciousness in response to an insistent rapping on his cabin door.

They'd been up until almost dawn catching up with the crew. What had started out as a formal debriefing devolved quickly into an awestruck question and answer session about the details of The Dragon's household, and from there, fell into ribald storytelling only mildly embellished beyond the bare facts.

There had, of course, been a fair amount of good-natured ribbing over the captain's arrival with a new beau in tow, but Hathar had deflected by inviting any of his crew who cared to to venture back and enter the palace to fetch a treasure of his own. Elin had taken it all in stride, relieved simply to be among friendly faces and swiftly putting distance between themselves and The Dragon.

Thinking of Elin, Hathar had to check himself, to make sure that what he thought was true was not just a cruel trick of his half-awake mind.

No, Elin was there, still fully abandoned to sleep, his golden lashes glinting on his cheeks in the slanting late-morning light.

The rapping came again, and Hathar heaved himself up, arranging the sheets for decency.

"Enter," he called, trying to make himself heard through the door, but keep from waking Elin.

It was Daren, the mate, and he was carrying what appeared to be a sodden chunk of wood.

"I'm sorry cap'n; I know you've had a rough stretch, but I thought you might want to see what we just fished out of the drink." He held out the thing in his hands, presenting it to Hathar as if it had some significance.

It *was* wood, and it was badly charred as well as wet. One area near the middle was only blackened with soot, and he could make out a faint impression there. He rubbed at it a bit with his finger and revealed some paint, a swirl of green on white. Turning the piece in the light, he was able to make out the pattern of the green paint through the soot. It looked like *nt Mi*.

He gave himself a moment, trying to goad his sluggish brain into providing an explanation for why this piece of flotsam seemed familiar.

All at once it struck, and Elin nearly shot out of the bed at the sudden sound of his howls of mirth.

Hathar pressed the piece of wood toward the now-awake Elin, still shaking with laughter and unable to speak.

Elin examined it, bleary and uncomprehending, looking from Hathar to Daren seemingly in hope that someone might explain the joke to him.

Daren looked uncertain, as if it might not be his place to speak, but he finally took pity on Elin and offered, "It's a piece of the dinghy. The one the captain used to row to shore."

This gave Hathar the grip on words he needed, and he managed to sputter out, "She burned my boat!"

Elin gave this all a second to percolate and then ventured, "A ship can carry a boat, but—"

Hathar cut him off with an emphatic, "Exactly!" and his laughter redoubled.

"So she really did do it, she just...didn't know you had a ship too."

"You've got it!" Hathar was breathing easily now. "I should have that engraved somewhere: I didn't know he had a ship too."

Elin was beaming now, infected by Hathar's mirth.

"Thank you Daren, for bringing this matter to my attention," Hathar said, still barely containing his glee. "You're dismissed, and we'll be on deck shortly."

As Daren shut the door behind him, Hathar rolled to pounce on Elin, pinning him playfully to the sheets and peppering him with kisses.

"Not too shortly though," he murmured. "What good is it to be captain if you can't make good use of your mate?"

About the Author

RL Mosswood lurks in the depths of the Pacific Northwest rainforest, where they dabble in queer fiction in an attempt to add a little magic to their otherwise mundane existence.

Email: mosswoodauthor@gmail.com

Twitter: @RL_Mosswood

Website: http://www.rlmosswood.com

Also Available from NineStar Press

www.ninestarpress.com